Desert Vengeance

Would such a hard-bitten, cold-hearted son of a
bitch get him free of the dirt that felt like it was
crushing him slowly to death? Pyle wondered.

"Ask you something, mister?" Pyle asked Edge.

"Sure."

"You are gonna help me out of this, ain't you?"

"Depends."

"On what, mister?" Pyle swallowed hard as a
flare of anger competed with fear and put a shrill
note into his voice.

Edge's ice-blue eyes raked the man's face, as if
his gaze would pierce the skull of the man buried
neck-deep in the desert earth.

"On what you did to get into that kind of a
hole . . ."

Other titles in the **EDGE** series from Pinnacle Books

#49

EDGE

REVENGE RIDE

BY

George G. Gilman

PINNACLE BOOKS   NEW YORK

EDGE #49: REVENGE RIDE

Copyright © 1985 by George G. Gilman

A Pinnacle Books edition, published by special arrangement with
New English Library.

First printing/May 1985

ISBN: 0-523-42268-7

Printed in the United States of America

PINNACLE BOOKS, INC.
1430 Broadway
New York, New York 10018

9 8 7 6 5 4 3 2 1

for
M.L.
One book for a lady who
has sent me so many

REVENGE RIDE

Chapter One

IT WAS hot as hell but a lot less crowded in Dry River Valley as Edge looked down at the small adobe house beside the trail. The broiling borderland sun was near the high point of its arc across the cloudless sky, and as the half-breed started his chestnut gelding down the valley's eastern slope, he had no reason to think he was still not alone in this desolate piece of southwestern New Mexico Territory.

But when he rode to within three hundred feet of the sand-gray-colored single-story house, he saw that the trio of buzzards perched on a stretch of new fencing at the side of the old building were not the only other living creatures in the vicinity. He was still on the gentle slope above the valley floor as he reined in his mount and from this elevated vantage point was able to see over the top of the painted three-rail fence the scavengers were poised on. Then, as the horse vented a soft whinny of uneasiness, the birds took to squawking

1

flight, the lumbering clumsiness of their takeoff acting to emphasize their rage of frustration. The man who was buried up to his neck in a corner of the recently fenced area twisted his head around to find out what had caused the birds to end their long and silent vigil.

Edge could see that the man had done a great deal of crying. The tracks of his old tears were clearly defined across his dirt-grimed cheeks. His blue-green eyes seemed to be totally drained of all moisture as their gaze darted from the vacated perch to the birds in flight and then to the horse and rider. At first his contorted features continued to display a sure and certain belief that the ugly birds were about to attack his living flesh, but then he squeezed his dry eyes tightly closed for part of a second and did a long double take toward the half-breed who heeled the gelding forward. An ecstatic grin abruptly spread across his face at the same time as he vented a sob that suggested his throat was as arid as his eyes. He was not yet entirely dehydrated, though, for beads of sweat began to squeeze from the pores of his face and on the hairless dome of his head as the rider came down onto the level stretch of trail that ran past the house. It was obviously not easy for the buried man to keep grinning as he slowly turned his head to watch the slow-riding man, whose own expression seemed to reflect a brand of spitefully callous dispassion.

"Mister!" the man trapped in the dirt blurted, shouting too loudly from out of his parched throat. "Mister, you just ain't gonna ride on by and leave me like this?"

The constricting fear of this prospect acted to moderate his tone. Then he sighed his relief and ran the tip of his parched tongue between his bone-dry lips as he saw the newcomer rein his horse to a halt again just a few feet away on the other side of the fence between the trail and the property.

"Ain't going to just ride on by, that's for sure, feller," Edge replied evenly as he swung lazily down from the saddle, flexing muscles that were stiff from a long ride. "Need to rest my horse for a spell. And this looks like the best spot in a big piece of country to do that."

The man with just his head and a short length of neck showing at the center of a patch of newly dug parched dirt now saw that he had been wrong in his initial judgment of the half-breed's attitude toward him. He was just a naturally unemotional individual for whom life held few, if any surprises. In repose—and the half-breed had evidently seen nothing in this area of Dry River Valley to shake him loose from such a well-balanced state of mind—his features were effortlessly set in an expression of coldly uncommunicative impassivity.

"Name's Pyle, mister."

"A pile of something is about what I took you for when I first saw you from back up the trail," Edge answered as he unlatched the five-bar gate in the new fence and led his horse through.

"Guess that even if you came up with a new joke about my lousy name, I'd find it tough to raise a laugh. Delmar Pyle is the whole thing."

"Been called Edge and nothing else for a long time, feller. And there's hardly anything that makes me laugh."

"I had you figured as a serious-type guy." Pyle had managed to suck up some lubricating saliva into his throat, and his voice had a less rasping tone now. The strain of craning his head around to watch what Edge was doing had become not worth the effort. "Me, I'm the happy-go-lucky kind. Under normal circumstances you understand. Ain't nothin' normal about this, that's for sure."

The corral was at the north side of the house, but Delmar Pyle was buried at a corner of the enclosure that would not be in shade until the blisteringly hot sun sank behind the ridge of the valley's western slope. The flat-roofed adobe building cast just a scant area of shadow across a part of the corral as the sun passed its noon peak, but this was supplemented by a temporary shelter formed some fifteen feet away by a sheet of burlap stretched between two rafters jutting out of the windowless adobe side wall and two poles driven into the dirt. There was an empty pail and the scattered remains of a hay bale on the dusty dirt at the base of the wall in the hot shade of the burlap sheet. The gelding sniffed noisily in the dry bucket but seemed reasonably content to chomp on the hay as Edge unfastened the cinch and dragged the saddle off the back of the animal.

"I figure Dry River Valley is a name that means just what it says, Pyle," the half-breed asserted as he dropped the saddle and unhooked the pair of canteens from around the horn.

"Folks at Wildwood say it's more than ten years since there was surface water running down the creek," the man in the dirt answered as he continued to face toward the northwest. There was an even more distinct intonation in his voice now, though, and it was not necessary to see his expression to know that he had returned to the despair he'd been feeling before he saw Edge. "There's some Mexicans that have been around here a whole lot longer than the Americans. They say there's plenty of water down under the dirt of the valley. That's why the women had me diggin' this hole

4

the damn bitches near buried me alive in, mister. Hoped to make a well here.''

"Wildwood's not so far from here, I guess.''

"Three miles. You could see it if the valley didn't swing to the east the way it does. They got a couple of deep wells there if you need to refill your canteens.''

"Obliged,'' Edge said, and poured some water into the pail, just enough for the gelding to moisten his mouth and rinse the dust out of his throat.

The sound of the water gurgling out of the neck of the canteen and splashing against the metal of the pail was almost too tantalizing for Delmar Pyle to resist. But he was able to check what would have been a snarl of embittered rage as he craned his head to look at the half-breed now. He saw there was nothing about the demeanor of the newcomer to suggest Edge was enacting a malicious charade to intensify his suffering. The expression on the half-breed's face was as impassive as always as he turned from tending his horse and stepped out from the shade of the burlap sheet. Surely his features would have worn a cruel grin of evil pleasure if he intended to taunt the helpless captive.

Edge didn't close his own canteen as he dropped down on his haunches in front of the buried man's head and used his teeth to draw the stopper from the neck of the companion container. Edge didn't tilt the second one to his lips to drink until after he had held the first canteen so Pyle could suck from it without danger of choking on a rush of water. Even so, the blue-green eyes continued to emanate a look of suspicion, as if he expected the canteen to be wrenched maliciously away before he had sipped his fill of its contents.

Edge estimated the age of Pyle at something below the midthirties, which meant the man had lost much of his hair prematurely. With a full head of the curly jet-black hair that now grew only in a horseshoe from temple to temple, he might not look out of his twenties. He had a pleasant but characterless face, basically round and a little overfleshy, which maybe suggested that his presently hidden torso and limbs were far from lean. He was clean-shaven, and unless he had an exceptionally light beard, he had probably shaved only this morning. He had fine white teeth unstained by the juice or smoke of tobacco and a clear and relatively unlined complexion that was evenly bronzed by long exposure to the elements. Only the skin of his skull, customarily protected by a hat, was reddened by the assault of the glaring morning sun.

"Thanks seems a lousy little word for how I feel about what you're doing, mister," Pyle said as gratitude drove mistrust from his clear-eyed gaze as Edge came up off his haunches and pressed the bungs into both canteens.

"Figure a man in your position wouldn't think it in his best interest to lie about there being plenty of water just three miles down the trail," the half-breed replied as he draped the thong that linked the pair of canteens over his shoulder. As he moved away from Pyle's head, he took some trouble to see that he did not kick dust in the face of the helpless man. He went to the front fence of the corral and leaned his forearms on the top rail as he looked along most of its length and across the facade of the house toward the south where the valley narrowed and made a sharp turn to the east. It was perhaps a mile and a half to the point where the valley became almost a canyon, the flanking ground rising higher as it got steeper and rockier.

"There's water a lot closer than that, mister," Pyle

countered as he eased his neck by abandoning the unnecessary effort at twisting his head to watch the man at the fence. "A couple of barrels right here in the house. And if you're hungry, there's grub in there too."

"None of it yours, I figure," Edge suggested as he took some makings from a shirt pocket and, maintaining his easy attitude against the fence, rolled a cigarette.

"Everythin' hereabouts is owned by Dinah and Harry," Pyle growled as if he was about to spit. But he remembered in time that he was in no condition to wantonly squander body fluids.

"You made mention of women wanting you to dig a well here," the half-breed pointed out as he raked his gaze over the terrain to the east and west and north of the old house and new corral. From down here on the valley floor, the country looked no more appealing than it had from up on the ridge where the Lordsburg-to-Wildwood trail emerged from the high peaks of the Animas Mountains and meandered through the borderland foothills that sprawled out of the United States territories and spilled southward into the Sonora and Chihuahua regions of Mexico. Up close, the dusty soil and scattered pieces of rock, the treeless slopes of the valley sides, the meagerly distributed thickets of gnarled vegetation and the line of pebbles that marked the course of the Dry River lacked the austere beauty that even barren desolation can sometimes convey when viewed from a distance.

"I ain't in no position nor do I have any reason to lie about somethin' like that, mister," Pyle answered, more embittered. "Talkin' about Dinah McCall and Harriet Newton. Women, both of them. And ain't no mistakin' that's what they are from the way they're built. But shortenin' her name from Harriet to Harry ain't the only way the Newton bitch tries to make out she ain't no woman.'' He twisted his head around to gaze at the half-breed as Edge struck a match on the fence rail to light the cigarette. ''I been around some, mister. And I seen this kind of crazy arrangement between two females before. I don't know if you—''

Edge dropped the dead match into the dirt and said, ''Known a few men's men. Heard about the kind of women who never go to balls to do their dancing.''

Delmar Pyle nodded within his imposed limits, a thoughtful expression on his tear-stained and sweat-run face as he studied for long seconds the quiet-spoken, laconic, and sardonic man who was in no rush to relieve the suffering of a fellow human being. Then a return of the ache in his neck forced him to look away. But in his mind's eye the impatient man in the dirt continued to hold a vivid impression of the half-breed.

And half-breed he distinctly was—white American for sure and, Pyle had thought at first, part Indian. But he had since revised his opinion. It was a Mexican strain in his bloodline that had given this guy the dark-hued complexion that would not have been light colored even if he had never experienced the extremes of weather over more than forty years. His jet-black hair was doubtless a part of his Hispanic heritage too. The thick way it grew and the manner in which he chose to wear it— long and unkempt to the shoulders at the sides and back—had tempted Pyle into the mistaken first impression of a half-breed Indian. But there was nothing of the Indian about the slitted eyes of ice-blue beneath hooded lids, the aquiline nose between high cheekbones, and the wide and thin-lipped mouth above the jutting jawline. All these features of the lean, time-lined face were from a mixing of Latin and Aryan blood.

His build was as lean as his facial features. He stood at least three inches taller than six feet, and some two hundred pounds of weight was evenly distributed over his frame. He was attired almost entirely in black powdered with the grays and reds of trail dust—a Stetson hat, kerchief, shirt, pants, and riding boots that he wore inside the cuffs of his pants. His gun belt and tied-down holster were also black, with a six-shooter in the holster and spare shells in every loop of the belt. Only a string of dull-colored beads around his throat relieved the travel-stained solid blackness of his garb. This necklet constituted Edge's sole affectation in an otherwise entirely functional outfit—unless there could be included in this category the Mexican-style mustache amid a half day's growth of heavy bristles.

Everything about the man added up to a drifting loner well able to take care of himself, who either could not afford or elected not to indulge himself in much beyond what was required to stay alive and to keep moving on.

Would such a hard-bitten, cold-hearted son of a bitch, Delmar Pyle wondered nervously as his eyes were again moistened by tears of trepidation, use the time and effort necessary to get him free of the dirt that felt like it was crushing him slowly to death?

"Ask you something, mister," Pyle said to end the long pause.

"Sure."

"You are gonna help me out of this, ain't you?"

"Depends."

"On what, mister?" He swallowed hard as a flare of anger competed with fear and put a shrill note into his voice.

"On what you did to get yourself into that kind of hole."

The sob he vented was another dry one, and as Delmar Pyle swung his head too fast, a grimace of pain momentarily masked the earnestness in his eyes as they met Edge's glinting gaze.

"Not a damn thing, mister. I didn't do nothin'."

"We've already talked about the way you're in no position to lie, feller," the half-breed reminded him, and took the cigarette from the corner of his mouth so he could mop his sweat-beaded face with his kerchief.

Pyle found himself observing the other man closely. There was quite a lot of grayness amid the long black hair as well as mottling the dark stubble of Edge. The faded beads on the thong around the neck of the cold-eyed son of a bitch were so out of character with everything else about him they had to be more than just ornamentation. Edge looked at him like he was just another inanimate, unfeeling part of the whole lousy valley, like he was a piece of rock, a stunted mesquite, a ridgeline, or the heap of horse apples his head had seemed to be from a distance. The bastard was acting like it was no strange thing to find a guy buried in the dirt up to his neck and was half expecting somebody else to come riding into the valley to save him the trouble of having to handle the chore of unearthing him.

Delmar Pyle had to take several deep breaths to check his anger and frustration. But this only made the sense of being crushed even more potent.

"All right, I put that wrong, mister," he blurted, and looked away from the half-breed again. He found it easier to stay calm when he didn't see those glittering, cold-as-ice eyes sweep over him every now and then. "It wasn't my fault is what I mean. Not all of it. Like I said, the two women that moved into this place are really built the way females are supposed to look. And they ain't hard to look at in the face either. I've been working for them almost three weeks, and I knew from the day I started that, as fine lookin' as they are, I was only wanted by them to do the heavy work of gettin' the place into shape. I didn't like it so much, bein' a normal and I figure healthy guy beddin' down so close to two of the finest lookin'—''

Pyle broke off and felt compelled to look around again when he heard the half-breed move. Then he felt an involuntary grin spread across his face as he saw Edge heading for where the shovel leaned in the angle of the corral fence.

"Guess I'm normal and healthy that way too," the half-breed said in response to the tacit query in the eyes of the buried man. "The kind that's liable to do more than just look at a beautiful woman. Expect to maybe get put down, but not buried.''

Pyle nodded again, too vigorously this time, and banged his teeth together. "I did a whole lot of lookin', mister," he hurried to explain, eager to build on the chord of affinity that he had apparently struck with Edge. "While I was fixin' the house roof and the shutters, fencin' the corral and paintin' the timber, and diggin' this well.''

"How tall are you, feller?" Edge asked as he advanced on the man's head, the blade of the long-handled shovel resting on his shoulder.

"Five and a half feet," Pyle replied, head still twisted around and his happy grin threatened by mistrust as he considered possible motives for the question.

"And you're standing up down there?"

"Yeah, and I can feel that my hands are tied in back of me, mister." He now looked ready to snarl a stream of invective up at the man who was calmly smoking the

11

cigarette and casually surveying his surroundings, the shovel still canted to his shoulder.

Then Edge advised, "Best you turn to face the other way."

"Why?" Pyle swallowed hard, for he was sure that the man towering above him had taken a two-handed grip on the shovel in a manner that made it into a vicious weapon.

"Just because you're smaller than I am doesn't mean you have to get dirt tossed in your face, feller." He pushed the blade of the shovel into the ground and thrust it all the way down with his foot, about eighteen inches away from the vulnerable head of Delmar Pyle.

The buried man turned his face away from the wedge of dirt and cloud of dust raised by the levered blade of the shovel. He forced out in a croaking tone, "Hey, this is really—"

"Sure, it's real big of me, feller," the half-breed cut in as he displaced the first shovelful of easy-to-dig, recently dug dirt. "Just wish you were a smaller one. Two-and-a-half-feet-tall midget would have been good."

"If I was that, I wouldn't have gotten into this spot in the first place," Pyle countered. "See, that Dinah—Dinah McCall—well, mister, it's been gettin' plainer and plainer since I worked here for a week or so that she ain't sold on this woman-only partnership like Harry—Harriet Newton, dammit! High, wide, and handsome I ain't, Edge, but I figure I'm the only man that Dinah's been close to in one hell of a long time. But she's known men before, that's for sure. Been with them, I guess. She sure knew how to give me the come-on. Way she flashed the smiles, way she stood sometimes, way she'd toss her hair, and the way she'd say things that would be took two ways . . ."

Into Pyle's reflective pause, the slowly but deliberately working Edge growled through teeth clenched with effort, "If you keep working your imagination that way, feller, could be you'll help shift some dirt from in front of you."

The prospect of imminent freedom allowed the buried man the luxury of spitting against the ground a few inches away from his pursed lips. Then he snarled, "It wasn't no imagination at the time. She was doin' it to me, and she knew she was doin' it to me. And she wasn't just givin' me the hots for the hell of twistin' me up inside. She was hopeful of gettin' somethin' in return, Edge. And when she stepped outa the house this mornin' she was sweatin' so hard for it her nightgown was all wet and stickin' to her body. And she paraded like a two-dollar whore around the side of the house and into the shebang I'd rigged for me and the horses to sleep under.

"Only natural for me to make a pass at her. And she sure as hell wasn't about to give me the brush-off. Until that other bitch come stormin' outa the house, yellin' blue murder that I was a rapist. Shit, I never even had the time nor chance to lay a finger on that sweatin'-with-the-hots female."

"If you had, I wouldn't be shoveling dirt for you, feller," Edge said as he worked more cautiously, digging closer to the buried man. He had uncovered him down to shoulder blade level now and could see Delmar Pyle had been buried in his gray long johns.

"It's real good to have somebody believe what a guy's sayin', mister."

"For rape, I figure that kind of woman would have done more than just bury you up to your neck," the half-breed augmented.

13

This drew a grunt of resignation from Pyle before the man continued in an increasingly embittered tone, "It was like I said, and you'll see pretty soon, mister. I ain't high, wide, and handsome. But I ain't no yellow-bellied weaklin', neither. But when them two females came at me, one of them yellin' she only stepped out for some fresh air and the other cursin' me worse than a Boston whalin' man, well, mister, I guess I just didn't count on either of them knowin' just where to hit a man to take the steam outa him. Don't know which of them done what. Just that one sure kneed me real hard between the legs and the other landed somethin' harder than a fist behind my right ear. Got dark a whole lot faster than it does at night. And a whole lot blacker. Woke up sweatin' and hurtin' and cryin' like a baby. And scared, mister. I ain't never been made unconscious in my life before. Been scared a few times, but never like I was when I saw what them bitches had done to me before goin' off. Then, when those mean-looking buzzards started to perch on the fence, well, mister, I got so scared I just couldn't stop myself from—"

"Yeah, I can smell how scared you got, feller," Edge cut in as he tossed away the shovel and dropped down on his haunches behind Delmar Pyle. He reached into the hole he had dug to the man's waist level, where his wrists were lashed tightly together.

"I'm almost out now, huh?" Pyle asked, his tone rising with hard-to-control excitement as he felt the half-breed's clawed hands fasten strong grips under his armpits. "And I know the first friggin' thing I'm gonna do after you cut me free, mister."

"Anything you like, long as it's out of smelling range of me," Edge growled, teeth gritted for the most

strenuous effort yet as he started to straighten up, hauling evenly at Pyle's armpits.

"Gonna scratch myself all over, from the top of my
head to the underneaths of my toes. Ain't it friggin'
hell, the way a man itches in places he never did before
just as soon as he ain't in no position to scratch?"

As the half-breed strained to free him, Pyle hollered
as he suffered the pain of being stretched between the
brute strength of Edge and the seemingly unyielding
hold of the earth around his legs.

"Goddammit, it didn't oughtta be as friggin' tough
as this!" Pyle snarled, then vented a cry of pain that
turned into a yell of joy as he felt himself start to slide
up out of the dirt.

Edge experienced a less expansive sense of satisfaction as he tried to ignore the stink of Pyle's soiled
underwear. After dragging him completely clear of the
crater, Edge released his grip on his armpits and straightened up.

"Will you look at that," Pyle said breathlessly after
he had rolled onto his side and gazed down the length
of his long johns to his bare feet where a length of the
same rope used to bind his wrists behind his back had
been tied around his ankles. In addition, his ankles had
been tied to a heavy chunk of flat rock that had an-
chored him in the dirt of the corral. "Did those bitches
ever figure on me stayin' here!"

"Could have been worse," Edge told the man as the
half-breed reached into the long hair at the back of his
own neck and brought his hand back into view fisted
around the handle of an open straight razor.

"Yeah, they could have buried me headfirst, I guess,"
Pyle agreed. Then as soon as his wrists were cut free,
he embarked on a frenzy of ecstatic scratching.

"Or they could have tied the rock to some other part of you," the half-breed added as he came erect after cutting through the rope at Pyle's ankles. "Bearing in mind what you had in mind to do to—"

"Hey, mister, I hurt enough thereabouts anyways!" Pyle complained as he rose unsteadily to his feet, and massaged his bruised crotch.

Edge flicked the razor closed and slid it back into the pouch held at the nape of his neck by the beaded thong. Then he took from a shirt pocket the cigarette he had only partly smoked before he started the chore of digging out Delmar Pyle, and lit it with a match struck on the butt of his holstered Frontier Colt. He turned away from the stockily built man in the stinking long johns who was ministering to his injured parts with one hand while he raked at many more areas of his body with the clawed fingers of the other.

"You gonna ride on out now, mister?" Pyle asked anxiously, halting Edge in his move toward the house at the other side of the corral.

"Figure to use some of the women's two barrels of water to wash up first."

"Hey, those two are real neat and tidy around the house, and they just hate to have anyone mess with their stuff."

"If you plan to be around when they get back, feller, you can tell them it was me who—"

"Hell, take what you want, mister," Pyle cut in bitterly. "Those bitches owe me for what they done to me, and I owe you for helpin' me, Edge."

"Just some water to wash up with," Edge told him, turning toward the house again.

Pyle held back for a moment, then followed and went on in a harsher tone, "Ain't nothin' inside worth takin',

I figure." Then his voice became earnest. "I'm a natural-born gambler, mister. And one day I'm gonna win a real big pot. And when I do that, I swear to you I'll do my best to find out where you are and—"

"Don't make promises, feller," Edge cut in coldly, irritated that the foul-smelling man was intent on staying close to him. "They're like bad laws. Always getting broken."

Delmar Pyle had paused briefly back at the spot where he had been buried so that he could stoop and pick up the shovel discarded by Edge. Now he held back to allow a gap to open up between himself and the half-breed, a gap that was the same length as the shovel that he swung high into the sun-bright air in a double-handed grip. He brought the tool viciously down so that the flat of the blade smashed against the taller man's skull, crushing the crown of the Stetson between the unbending metal and the head beneath.

Edge took one more step, then fell heavily to his knees. He remained rigid for part of a second and pitched forward full length on the ground amid billows of disturbed dust. His hat rolled off his head.

For stretched seconds the silence was kept from being absolute only by the labored breathing of the man slumped across the ground. The one who had done the damage held his breath and remained poised to swing the shovel again if Edge should reveal by the merest sign that he was playing possum. But then, as the gray-streaked black hair on the top of the injured man's head began to get darkly wet, Delmar Pyle realized that the ragged breathing and stillness of the half-breed were not part of any voluntary pretense. The man called Edge was out cold—was perhaps even critically hurt by the force of the brutally struck blow. And for just a second, Pyle's

17

fear of immediate retaliation was replaced by remorse. But this feeling soon gave way to an elation that spread a broad grin across his characterless face. There was humor rather than rancor in his voice as he responded to the final comment of the now unconscious man:

"Not just promises and bad laws, mister. I can break heads too."

Chapter Two

EDGE REGAINED consciousness amid sounds not unlike some pitched battle.

As he lay, eyes closed, on a piece of sun-parched dirt, he found he was able to isolate and identify one sound against the deafening din of the background. This was a scream of rage being drawn out to breathless length. As he recognised it as his own scream, he knew that he was going to pay back with full interest the sneaky son of a bitch who had bushwhacked him.

He flickered his eyes open and the painful clamor in his mind receded as the glaring brightness of the hot sunlight swept over him.

"Yeah, the crazy fool is coming out of it, Dinah," a woman said tautly.

Edge fastened his mind on to the words and found he was able to keep his eyes open for progressively longer periods. The pain was harsher when he succeeded in doing this, but he decided keeping his eyes open preferable to the futile rage that refused to be appeased in the darkness filled with the deafeningly loud imaginary sounds.

"Do you think he'll die, Harry? I don't think I've ever seen so much blood on a person before." The woman's voice expressed a mixture of apprehension and revulsion.

Edge blinked a great deal, but this did not close his glittering slits of eyes long enough to have his mind play any more tricks on him.

"I'll tell one of you ladies what I know," he rasped through gritted teeth.

One of them gasped and the second blurted, "Oh, my good Lord!"

He was too deeply preoccupied with the excruciating pain under his skull to decide which of them spoke and which expelled her breath. "Don't just *think*; I know for sure that if the lady with the gun aimed at me ever points it at me again and doesn't kill me, I'll kill her."

He was not able to check the groan that demanded bursting exit from his throat as he completed the move he struggled to make while he strung together with punishing difficulty the words of the threat, the sound rasping through clenched teeth and between pursed lips as he rolled heavily onto his back. For long moments he screwed his eyes tightly shut as the glaring sun blazed blindingly down on them. But there was no barrage of earsplitting sounds in the darkness now. Just the voice of Dinah McCall repeating, "Oh, my good Lord."

Harriet Newton vented a peal of laughter that sounded both forced and false, which she abruptly curtailed when she saw Edge roll his head to the side so that when he reopened his eyes again, he was no longer staring up at the dazzlingly bright sky.

"How are you going to manage that, creep?" the Newton woman taunted. "Going to talk me to death, are you?"

They stood close together, side by side, some six feet away from him just inside the corral at the open gateway. The one with the Winchester angled from her hip was a redhead, the other one a brunette. Both were dressed in work clothes more suited to men but both, just as Delmar Pyle had said, were unmistakably women in the way their forms filled out their clothing. Edge took no more notice of them than this before he lengthened the focus of his slitted eyes and saw clearly the flatbed wagon with two horses in the traces that stood on the trail outside of the fence and open gate. And in retrospect, he could identify the loud sounds that had earlier been distorted by his mind coming to brutal consciousness.

Hoofbeats and clattering wheel rims. Creaking timbers and groaning springs. The jingle of harness rings and the snapping of leather. Voices raised in surprise and perhaps fear. The thud of footfalls. The metal-on-metal scrapings of the rifle's repeating action being pumped. And his own involuntary cry of pain or anger or a mixing of the two.

"Two questions," he said through a grimace as he brought the women into sharp focus again.

"I got a whole lot more than that for you, creep," the Winchester-toting redhead snapped.

"Oh, for Pete's sake, Harry," Dinah chided.

"First one is to *ask* you to point the rifle someplace else. Nothing personal against you, lady. I just don't like anybody to aim a gun at me, and I try to warn folks once before—"

"There!" Dinah said with determination as she reached

out, gripped the barrel of the rifle firmly, and pushed it so it was angled toward the sky.

"Do you mind!" her partner snarled, and jerked the Winchester angrily free of the fisted grasp. But then she held it in a two-handed grip across the base of her belly, the hammer still back but the muzzle directed toward the dirt.

"Obliged," Edge said softly, and gave a look of mild curiosity to the angrily grimacing redhead and the intrigued brunette. "Second one: was it me screaming loud enough to wake the dead that brought you ladies racing up the trail home?"

"Why, we didn't drive any faster than a steady walk the whole way from town," Dinah answered quickly. "What with the heat and the way the dust rises so."

"Wouldn't make no never mind if you was blubbering like a brat that got his candy stole," the Newton woman cut in caustically, "far as she and me are concerned. Hard as rock or weak as kittens, we couldn't care less about men in general or you in particular. But you can quit worrying about it yourself. If you thought you were hollering, that's all you did—thought it. It was real admirable the way you came awake to all that pain. The way you did it, so quiet and without no fuss and all. Well, it showed a couple of mere women just what a tough and brave—"

"Cut it out, Harry," Dinah growled.

"Again I'm obliged," Edge said, and made it plain with an impassive glance that he was grateful for the information given by Harriet, rather than to Dinah for the interruption. This after he had struggled to get his head and back up off the dirt and discovered he could sustain the splay-legged seated attitude as long as he braced himself with one hand a little way behind him.

With the other hand he explored the damage to the top of his head and felt a great deal of congealed blood matting his hair and a scalp gash running front to back that seemed to his probing fingertips to be immensely long and broad and deep. But the ache was no longer unbearably intense inside his head, the wound was tender rather than searingly painful, his vision was only impaired when he moved his head too suddenly, and he was no longer hallucinating over sounds that did not exist. He reached for the shovel that had done the damage and used it as a crutch as he got to his feet.

While he did this, he kept his eyes closed and concentrated on a vivid mental image of Delmar Pyle. It was his determination to even the score with the man who had laid him out, rather than his pain and weakness, that carved the scowl on his face. His expression of hate caused Dinah McCall to stop short in her tracks as she made a move to go to his aid, while Harriet Newton's acid contempt for the half-breed's masculinity became harder set.

"Oh, my good Lord," the brunette gasped as Edge stood at his full height and the glinting threads of cruel ice-blue beneath the hooded lids intensified.

"Ain't he something, though?" the redhead growled, and spat expertly to the side.

But when he took a first step toward the women, they were equally fast and afraid, and backed off from him. Then he veered a little to the side of the open gateway in which they stood and reached for and took a grip on the length of fence closest to him. A grin of achievement displaced the scowl on his sweating face as he leaned comfortably against the timber and dropped the shovel.

"No sweat, ladies," he offered in an even tone. He

delved into a pocket of his shirt for the makings and eyed them with an element of appraisal for the first time.

They were a match for height, both a little less than five and a half feet tall. The black-haired Dinah McCall was the younger of the two, with the kind of fresh-faced look that made it difficult to estimate her actual age. Perhaps she was in her early twenties, or she could be close to thirty. She was also the heavier, but she was by no means fat. Her generously curved body was probably more noticeably overdeveloped in contrast with the angular slenderness of the woman at her side. Her sun-bronzed face was round and her complexion was flawless. Her features were softly curved in a way that made her a pretty girl rather than a beautiful young woman. This was emphasized by the style in which her silken hair tumbled far below her shoulders at both back and front in a series of smooth waves. Too, her light blue eyes were bright with a quality of childlike innocence rather than keen intelligence. Despite the obvious manner in which her flared hips were contoured by the blue denim of her work-stained pants and the sensuous shape of her large breasts clearly outlined by the tight fit of the sweat-dampened gray shirt, the clothing gave Dinah McCall the look of a tomboy. And even if she had been dressed in an entirely feminine style, Edge reflected absently, she had the kind of cherubic face that would still cancel out her shape so that she would look like a child masquerading as a woman. Much like Delmar Pyle, her features lacked any character-defining qualities.

On the other hand, thirty-five years of hard living had stamped their mark on the face of Harriet Newton. Her experience was evident in the cool gaze of her pale green eyes, the faintly sardonic set of her mouth, and the just perceptible tracery of cynical wrinkles at the sides of her eyes and lips. There was a quality of undeniable sexual attractiveness about her lean, weathered face that was closer to being homely than handsome. With carefully applied paints and powders and a less severe style to her straight, short-cropped auburn hair, the woman could have made nonsense of this judgment by the half-breed.

The angular bone structure of her face was matched by that of her body. Her shoulders were square, her breasts distinctly conical, her belly flat, and her hips less curvaceously pronounced than those of the woman who stood beside her. Her pants and shirt did not fit her so tightly as did those of Dinah McCall. And she wore an old Army forage cap with the badge removed. In addition to the rifle she continued to clutch tightly in both hands, she had a Remington Army model revolver thrust into a holster held on her right hip by a belt that was meant only to keep her pants from falling down.

Dinah McCall was not armed.

And neither, Edge was unsurprised to discover, was he. His holster was empty and the booted Winchester was gone, along with his saddle and the rest of his gear. Pyle had, of course, stolen the chestnut gelding. Edge felt the flatness of his hip pocket without delving inside for the bankroll that had been in there before he was knocked out. It was as an afterthought that he reached into the hair at the nape of his neck and found out the acquisitive bastard had even snitched the straight razor.

"From where I stand, the creep left you just the clothes you stand up in," the Newton woman said coldly, with a faint trace of quiet enjoyment in her tone.

"Which you figure serves me right, huh?" he answered evenly.

The redhead shrugged her square shoulders, seemed on the point of admitting her pleasure at his losses, but then decided she didn't feel as good about it as she thought she might. She accused him coolly, "You set the little shit free."

He nodded, taking care to move his dully throbbing head slowly. "It seemed to be the right thing to do at the time, lady."

"He tell you why we did that to him, tough guy?"

Edge felt confident enough of his ability to maintain his balance to leave the support of the fence and go to where his crushed hat lay in the dust.

"That he tried to screw one of you ladies even though he knew the kind you were." He lowered himself onto his haunches rather than bend down to retrieve his hat. There was a bad moment after he came upright again when Dry River Valley took a violent tilt under his feet and darkness gathered, but the heat of the sun soared to scorching heights again and he regained enough control of his senses to get the drift of what Harriet Newton was saying to him.

". . . excuses for our sexual proclivities. Pyle didn't lie. He did attempt to take liberties with Dinah and—"

"And he made it worse for himself by accusing me of inviting his filthy interest," the younger woman hurried to add.

"That's right."

"And it seems to me," Dinah went on earnestly, "that there are a lot worse things we could have done to him. As it was, we just wanted to make him sweat some. Figured to dig him out and set him free ourselves soon as we got back from town."

Edge reshaped his Stetson and set it back on his head. As soon as the split in his scalp was shaded from the hot sun, the wound felt less sore. He struck a match on a thumbnail to light the cigarette hanging at the corner of his mouth.

"But we'd have took care to run him off the place empty-handed before he could do—"

"Harry, we'd better see if he took any of our stuff!" Dinah cut in, suddenly anxious. And at a nod of agreement from the redhead, she turned out of the corral gateway and hurried toward the house. Her voluptuous hips and rear rolled with a guileless naturalness that Edge found difficult to ignore.

"She doesn't do that on purpose!" Harriet Newton snapped, and glowered as she recaptured his impassive attention. "Dinah just can't help the way she moves. Which is something I took into account when I said we should bury Pyle to his neck and give him time to think about what he almost done to her."

"Even if she didn't happen to be your type, she ain't mine, lady," Edge said.

The woman continued to glower at him for stretched seconds, as if she was seeking to penetrate the inscrutable mask to find out if there was an implied insult in the flatly spoken response. But then the shrilly concerned voice of her partner curtailed the scrutiny.

"Harry! Harry! Come see what he's done! Oh, my good Lord! After all the time and trouble we took to fix up the place!"

Harriet Newton heard the quavering voice with anxiety. She looked ready to burst into tears of her own when Dinah suddenly vented a sob of misery. But then she regained her self-control, and as she moved to see what had so upset the other woman, she flung back at Edge, "You've proved to yourself that you can walk without

27

falling down, tough guy. So why don't you walk the hell away from here?"

Dinah continued to yell for the older woman to hurry to the house, lacing the demands for haste with some crude imprecations at the long-gone Delmar Pyle. Against the barrage of words that spurred Harriet Newton into a loping run, Edge growled resolutely, "Figure to, lady. Soon as I know which way to go."

And it didn't take him too much time to locate evidence that showed the direction Pyle had gone on the stolen chestnut gelding.

It could have been Wildwood, for there were hoofprints to show where he had ridden off the trail immediately opposite the house. His tracks angled across the slope to the southeast, along a line that looked as if it could be a shortcut to avoid the swing in the trail into the canyonlike gorge.

It was much quieter in the house as Edge found what he was looking for and stood at the side of the trail, smoking the cigarette as he gazed impassively in the direction Delmar Pyle had gone. Dinah was weeping softly and the older, stronger woman occasionally spoke placatingly to her. Less often she said something in a harsh tone which was obviously directed toward the man who occupied the half-breed's thoughts. Edge heard the woman's voice without having the inclination to listen to the words she spoke. Instead, he silently contemplated the desolate, sun-baked side of Dry River Valley and showed no hint by his expression that he was anticipating with keen pleasure the prospect of killing a man. And, in truth, if anyone saw the way his thin lips sometimes drew back to expose his gritted teeth and the way the glinting light in the narrowness of his ice blue eyes grew colder, they were likely not to realize that this cruel grin was actually his grimaced response to a fresh wave of pain surging through his head.

"Oh, my good Lord, I'm going to be sick to my stomach. I know I am!" These words rang out clearly as Dinah rushed into the doorway of the house and stood on the threshold, taking gulping breaths of the hot air of early afternoon. "You should come see what that . . . that swine has done to our beautiful little home!" she urged breathlessly as she quelled her nausea and saw Edge standing on the other side of the trail.

He dropped the cigarette butt into the dust and crushed out its fire beneath a heel as he turned and started toward the woman who was sagged against one of the doorjambs. She was looking younger than ever now that her pretty, plump face was puffed and blotched and wet from crying.

"It took us so long and so much hard work to make it nice," she moaned miserably as she backed off the threshold to allow him entrance.

"A hard-as-rock tough guy like him won't care about that kinda—" Harriet Newton began to growl. She stood in the doorway with her back to Edge and didn't know he had accepted the other woman's distraught invitation until she sensed his presence and snapped her head around.

"You're a strange lady, because that's how nature made you," he told her evenly as he halted on the threshold. "Maybe I'm harder and tougher than the average feller because that's what life's made me be. Outside of that, we don't know a thing about each other. And guessing is for games no one's in the mood to play in this parlor right now, seems to me."

The leaner, older, less pretty but more sensual woman

was briefly angered by the soft-spoken put-down. Then she was embarrassed and finally contrite. Harriet came close to voicing an apology, but long ingrained prejudice rebelled against the impulse, and she joined Dinah and Edge in scanning the wrecked room. She made the rasping vow, ''That little shit is gonna pay for this.''

The adobe house was old, but the door and the window shutters had been recently repainted, the roof patched, and the exposed ends of the rafters newly treated with oil-smelling preservative. The element-ravaged exterior of the old adobe house offered no clue to the stylish creature comforts that were to be found inside its stained and crumbling walls. Had been there, anyway, before the vengeful Delmar Pyle had set about striking back at the women for their humiliating treatment of him.

Edge had spoken of a parlor because there was no other word to describe the very American room in this most Mexican style house on to which the doorway gave. It was overcrowded with large, heavy furniture of oak and walnut and mahogany, the timber dark stained and highly polished. Included were a round table and four side chairs, a Pilgrim chest, two winged armchairs, a long-case clock, a lowboy, and a desk and bookcase. There were deep pile rugs on the dirt floor and a host of pictures and samplers hanging on the whitewashed walls. Fine porcelain jugs and plates and figurines had been displayed on a shelf that stretched along three walls on the room, a foot below the ceiling, but every finely crafted and decorated item had been smashed, and each piece of upholstered furniture had been slashed. Each lovingly polished surface was now deeply gouged. Most of the volumes had been hurled out of the bookcase and many were torn apart. The glass of the bookcase doors was shattered and more shards of broken glass had been spread across the floor when the tall clock was sent crashing down. Paint—white like that which had been used on some sections of the corral fence—was wantonly splashed over the rugs and across those pieces of furniture too heavy to move and too ornately carved to submit easily to the gouging effect of a gunsight or a carving knife.

"That's our bedroom through there," Dinah said, and it was impossible to tell without looking at her whether rage or bitterness or the threat of more tears caused her voice to tremble. On the periphery of his vision, Edge saw her shaking hand raised to point to a doorway where he had only a narrow view of a room that seemed to be furnished in a brighter style than this one. "He smashed all our bottles in there. Scattered all our powders. Used our rouge and our lip colorings to scrawl on the walls. And he piled all our prettiest clothes on the bed and set fire to . . ."

She was forced to leave off the description of destruction as the strength of her emotions gathered to choke off her words.

"He made sure to put the fire out, though," Harriet Newton added. "Figure he didn't want the whole place to burn down so we couldn't see the trouble he went to."

"And in the kitchen . . ." the younger woman blurted, waving her outstretched hand toward the only other doorway. "In our kitchen he did disgusting things in the skillets and the pans and—"

"All right, baby, we can all smell what he did in our kitchen," Harriet interrupted her partner, who sounded close to hysteria as she babbled the words out of her constricted throat. As Harriet spoke, the more self-controlled redhead picked her way cautiously through the debris to get to the kitchen door and close it. With her back to the door, the repeater rifle held across the base of her flat belly again, she raked her gaze once more over the vandalized room in which the adobe-cooled air once again smelled only of spilled paint. She said dully, "For sure he's gonna pay for this."

Only the way her knuckles showed white from the tightness of her grip on the Winchester revealed the extent of her determination to carry out the threat. In her tone of voice, the expression on her tight-fleshed face, and her less than upright stance against the door was exhaustion and dejection. She was physically and emotionally drained of everything but the steadfast resolve to seek revenge, and this was the only prop that was keeping her from collapse.

"You bet he's going to do that, Harry!" Dinah assured her earnestly, and started purposefully across the wrecked room, not caring about the fragments of china and glass that she trod into tinier pieces and ground further into the paint-stained rugs.

Edge warned coldly, "If you get to him first, you better leave some for me."

"Hey!" the redhead yelled as Edge left the room.

"Let him go, Harry!" the younger woman urged as she followed the redhead out of the coolness of the house and into the blistering afternoon.

"Hey, you!" the redhead yelled again.

Edge halted on the other side of the trail and gestured across the valley slope to the southeast. "He took off that way. In my saddle, on my horse, and with my guns and gear. And when he needs to, he'll pay his way with my money."

He rasped the back of a hand along the bristles of his

jawline and spat a globule of saliva into an area of hoof-imprinted dust.

"You saw him leave?" Dinah asked, confused.

"Don't be silly, baby," the redhead chided absently, her attention fixed upon Edge. "He's a skilled tracker—isn't that right, Mr. . . . ?"

"I've had to do some tracking in my time, lady."

She nodded curtly, then gestured with her head across the barren slope. "The creep has taken the shortcut to town. It's pretty easy going on a horse. On foot, though, I'd say it's slower than riding the wagon on the trail. Especially in this heat if a man has a bad crack on the head and's lost a whole lot of blood."

"You offering me a job, lady?"

"It figures you need one."

"Harry, for Pete's sake, we know the way to Wildwood well enough!" Dinah McCall entreated, her bright blue eyes clouded by anxiety as she switched her gaze quickly between the redhead and the half-breed.

"Since you just said how he stole your money and your stuff, that'll take money to replace," Harriet continued.

"But we don't need him to help us get to—"

"Hush up, baby," the older woman murmured, maintaining her steady gaze on the impassive face of Edge. "Like I say, Wildwood is the first place you reach down in that direction, Mr. . . . ?"

"Edge," he supplied flatly.

"As in sharp?" She tried a smile that flickered and died.

"Sometimes dull, lady."

"But not now. You know Pyle isn't likely to stop over in town for very long. If at all. South of Wildwood is Sonora and the whole of Mexico. And who's to say south is the way the little shit will keep on going?''

"Oh, my good Lord," Dinah moaned as despondency displaced apprehension on her tear-ravaged face.

"Places to buy a horse and a gun and shells in the local town, lady?''

The square shoulders, no longer slumped, shrugged. "No traders or a gunsmith as such, Mr. Edge. But plenty of people willing to sell everything they own at the right price.''

"And you can afford what they'll ask for what I need?''

Harriet Newton nodded, and this time the smile flickered into life for a little longer as she answered, "There's a bank in Wildwood. Dinah and me have enough money in it to stake you to—"

"Whatever my costs, that'll be my pay for the job. Plus you take care of the eating supplies until we catch up with him. If he's still got my horse and guns in good shape, you get the ones I buy in Wildwood.''

The redhead pondered the conditions for a few moments, then gave one of her curt nods and rested the Winchester barrel on her left shoulder as she strode across the trail, her right hand extended. "Agreed,'' she proclaimed as the half-breed shook her hand.

Dinah McCall, who had been angrily coming to terms with the fact that arrangements were being made without consulting her, now demanded, "And if we do catch up with Delmar Pyle, what then?''

"Not if, baby. When!''

"All right—when!'' the younger woman submitted petulantly. "But the question's still the same.''

"I plan to kill him, lady.''

"And you and me are going to be there to watch, baby.''

"Watch? I don't just want to watch, Harry! I want to do it myself and—"

"That's how you feel now, baby," the redhead cut in. She moved back across the trail to be beside Dinah, and draped her free arm around her shoulders. "That's how we feel now, just a few minutes after we've seen what he did to our beautiful home. When I first saw the terrible thing he did, I could have easy killed him in a thousand ways right here and now. But when we find the lousy little shit, it'll be a lot of miles from here. It'll be a matter of killing the creep in cold blood then, baby. I know I couldn't do that, no matter how much I'm hating him right at this minute. And you neither. I'm sure of that, Dinah baby."

The round prettiness of the brunette's tear-stained face continued to be ruined by a sullen frown as she listened to the other woman and stared fixedly at Edge, who now began to amble toward the stalled flatbed and pair. Then she shook her head vigorously, but not in a gesture of dissent. For she announced, "All right, Harry. Okay, Mr. Edge. I can see how it might be that we'll need you."

The half-breed glanced over his shoulder at the couple standing side by side at the front of the house and saw that Harriet Newton was unashamedly relieved while Dinah McCall looked to be nervously anxious about the alliance.

"Sure, lady," he drawled in a tone of irony. "Even women like you got to allow there are some things that just have to be man handled."

Chapter Three

ONCE HE had checked over the two bay geldings and the wagon to which they were hitched, the half-breed agreed to go along with a number of suggestions made by the redhead. At first this was no hardship at all, since it was her idea that Dinah should boil up some water for cleaning the wound in his head and to make coffee. And then he sat in the shade of the burlap sheet at the side of the house, drinking the coffee and smoking a cigarette while the younger woman bathed his head with a degree of tender care that he found surprising in someone who seemed to become more tautly afraid of him the closer she got to him.

This odd couple of women had not only been diligent housekeepers around their place. The elderly flatbed and the horses that were past their prime were also in fine shape from skilled care. And from what he had seen of Harriet Newton's Remington revolver and Winchester rifle, the weapons looked to have been cleaned and oiled regularly. Now, as the brunette fixed up the blood-crusted split in his scalp, the redhead began to bring supplies out of the house and load them on the wagon: a water barrel and some sacks of feed for the geldings, a heap of blankets and a few pots and pans cleaned of what Delmar Pyle had put in them, a large carton in which cans and jars rattled together, and a wooden crate packed to overflowing with paper-wrapped items.

Harriet Newton was loading the wagon solely with essential supplies for what could be a long trip through barren and desolate country. The manner in which she carried the supplies out of the house and swung them aboard the wagon, then covered them with a sheet of burlap and lashed the whole thing down with ropes all served to underscore the fact that here was a physically strong and functionally capable woman.

"There, I'm done, Mr. Edge," Dinah announced suddenly as she straightened up from squatting behind him. "I can't properly bandage it in such an awkward place, but there's no festering yet and I guess if you keep it covered with your hat—"

"Obliged, lady," he interrupted her nervous explanation. "It feels a whole lot better for what you've done."

She nodded quickly, picked up the bowl of blood-tinted water, and emptied it on the parched ground beyond the patch of shade cast by the burlap. She did this as she hurried to leave the corral. In a moment she climbed the fence instead of using the gate because that method put distance between herself and the half-breed and brought her close to the redhead more quickly.

Watching the two of them as he took a final swallow of coffee and then sucked a last drag of smoke from the cigarette, Edge was struck by the unbidden notion that had he not known otherwise he would likely have taken the women for sisters. Then there rapidly followed another involuntary and inconsequential thought: that with a greater disparity of ages, the manner in which the women behaved toward one another could well lead a stranger to mistake them for mother and daughter.

With a just-audible grunt of irritation with himself, he dropped his cigarette butt into the dregs of his coffee and carefully set his hat back on his head before he rose to his feet. As he left the corral by way of the gate, he told himself that what the women might appear to be was of even less importance to him than what they were in terms of their relationship to each other. For the rest, they simply shared his need to extract vengeance from Delmar Pyle—and their wagon and horses, guns and supplies would make the vengeance hunt a little easier, more comfortable, and safer than it would otherwise have been.

He would have liked it better were the women to remain here so that he could head on down the trail alone, burdened with sufficient supplies for just his own needs. But with such women as these—particularly such a woman as Harriet Newton—that could only have been achieved by force, and using force would have put him in a league with Delmar Pyle.

"What the hell do you think you're doing, Edge!" the redhead demanded in a snarling tone, her voice cutting viciously in on his unruffled train of thought as he started to climb up on the wagon seat.

The younger woman was quick to warn shrilly, "Don't point the gun at him, Harry!"

Edge halted with one foot on a wheel spoke and turned just his head to look at the doorway of the house, where the women were side by side again, Harriet glowering and Dinah expressing fear.

"Fixing to leave," he said.

The brunette lowered her restraining hand when it was obvious the redhead was not about to draw the Remington from its holster.

"We're not ready yet," Harriet came back.

He completed the act of hauling himself up on the seat, then looked toward the women again and drawled as he began to unwind the reins from around the brake lever, "When you are, at least we won't have to waste even more time turning the rig around to head the way we want to go."

He let off the brake and with soft encouragement and gentle but firm use of the reins urged the geldings to come around in a half turn. He halted them when the front of the wagon was directly opposite the doorway in which the women stood. At close quarters he could see that Dinah remained afraid of what was happening, while Harriet now seemed strangely ill at ease beneath the surface of her diminishing anger, as if she was embarrassed by her overreaction to Edge's approach on the wagon.

"How were we to know? We thought you were just going to make off—"

"We made a deal, lady," the half-breed cut in evenly. "I've been happier about deals I've made in the past, but the only driving seat I'm in right now is on the wagon. Anytime I start getting tired of our deal, I'll give you fair warning."

"Well, that's all right then," the redhead said, too fast and sharp.

"We just have a few things to pack and bring with us," the younger woman added.

"One other thing," he said as they turned back into the house. "When I leave, it won't be with anything that doesn't belong to me. All I care about is gettin' the feller that did the wrong to me."

"You want me to say I'm sorry?" Harriet asked. "All right, I'm sorry I got you wrong. In future I'll do my very best to keep in mind that you're a man of honor, Mr. Edge." As if she considered her tone of cynicism insufficient, she added a scornful sneer to the apology.

"Something else you might keep in mind, lady."

Her expectant look was tinged with anticipation of an insult. At the same time Dinah tugged nervously on the older woman's arm, anxious that the needling exchange should come to a quick end.

"It's only real women who get the privilege of keeping a man waiting."

The redhead sucked saliva up into her mouth and spat it forcefully into the dust at her feet.

"I figure you sweat a lot too," Edge said evenly.

"Come on, Harry," Dinah urged, and let go her grasp on the other woman's arm as she swung back into the house. "It won't take long to finish up. And anyway, he's already said he won't steal the wagon and stuff."

The redhead grunted and gave him a look of triumph from her cool green eyes. Her attitude conveyed pride in her partner for showing an uncharacteristic flash of smart reasoning while at the same time challenging the man on the wagon seat to argue the point.

"Harry, come help me so we can get started!"

The redhead directed what was intended as a parting glance of contempt at Edge, but he drawled evenly, "Can see how you're the top hand in a lot of ways,

Harry. But in another, you're a whole lot more the female.''

Her scowl took a firmer hold and she spat again as he explained, ''The way she talks makes a hell of a lot of sense. And you just talk a hell of a lot.''

Chapter Four

THE CHESTNUT gelding that Delmar Pyle had stolen from Edge was hitched to one of a line of posts out front of the cantina down at the far southern end of Wildwood's single street.

It had been a tensely quiet trip over the three miles to town from the women's place out in Dry River Valley. The half-breed had driven, Harriet Newton had been hunched on the seat beside him, and Dinah McCall had ridden in the back of the wagon wedged between the burlap-draped freight and the large trunk that the women had insisted upon packing and loading before they would leave. In the trunk, the younger woman had felt it necessary to explain soon after Edge urged the two-horse team into an easy walk, were clothes, some books, a few pieces of inexpensive jewelry, and some porcelain ornaments. Nothing of any great value, but these treasured possessions were the only ones that had not been stolen or destroyed during Pyle's savage onslaught on the house.

Edge had merely nodded in stone-faced agreement with the brunette when she insisted it was wise not to leave such easy-to-steal property in an isolated house that could well be empty for many days. And then the long silence had begun as the tension Dinah had sought to ease started gradually to stretch tauter in the inert, blisteringly hot afternoon air.

The half-breed's head, which had hurt a lot less after the woman's tender attentions, now began to trouble him again. The wound hurt from every jar of a wheel over a bump in the trail.

And the prospect of failure to take his revenge against the man with the blue-green eyes and the horseshoe of black hair wound the spring of tension tighter inside the half-breed. But he remained expressionless and silent, and in that section of his mind where rational thinking was still possible, he continued to monitor his surroundings. However, he neither saw nor sensed the slightest sign of danger on the slow ride along the narrowing, curving valley of the Dry River. He was certain that the only eyes watching him were the light blue ones of Dinah McCall, which he felt fixing him with a look of keen and open interest whenever she thought he wasn't looking.

Which could mean she was not so much scared of him as afraid of how she herself felt about him, and anxious that he should not realize how he affected her. And, recalling what Delmar Pyle had said about how Dinah McCall had lured him . . .

In a short time the valley became a gorge, then began to curve southward and widen again. In the cliff-shaded air between the sixty-foot-high walls, he began to discern the distinct odor of woodsmoke laced with the appetizing aroma of cooking chili.

Just for a moment Edge felt hungry. Then he realized that the fragrant smoke came from more than one fire, and that it originated from a point close to three miles from the start of their wagon ride.

"Be Wildwood I can smell," he murmured.

"Don't it just stink to high heaven?" Dinah McCall sneered.

In a moment the redhead explained, "Something you maybe oughtta know, Edge. The people in town don't hold Dinah and me in very high regard. But it doesn't bother us one little bit. So you just concentrate on finding out all you can about the little shit who made a sucker out of you."

Dinah expressed a new brand of fear with a loud catch of her breath as the redhead directed a hard-eyed, side-long look at Edge. He met it briefly before he returned his attention to what lay ahead of the wagon and allowed, "Can't smack anyone in the mouth for telling the truth, lady."

The gorge came to an abrupt end as they came up to the town-limits marker, its branded lettering still readable but the numerals of its elevation long made indecipherable by the elements. The sign was in the form of a long plank stretched over the trail on two twenty-foot-high posts. It was sited a dozen feet or so from the end of the gorge, and it was perhaps a quarter mile in a straight line from here to the other end of the twisting street at the base of the hill. As he gazed down, Edge knew with instinctive certainty that the lone horse hitched out front of the distant building on the far side of town did not merely resemble his gelding; it was the actual horse Delmar Pyle had stolen from him.

"What's the last building at the far end of this street on the west side?" he asked in a tone he had to consciously keep from thickening as he steered the team under the limits marker, toward the first downward curve.

"The cantina," Dinah supplied in a rush. "It's run by a real brute of a man named Troy. He's one of the few Americans left in Wildwood. Harry and I don't drink hard liquor, so we've never had call to step inside. But it has an awful name among decent folks and—"

"Obliged."

"I take it you are a drinking man?" the older woman said sourly. "I'm not sure that we feel obligated to put up money for you to . . ."

She recognized that the hard look on his heavily bristled face was caused by something more serious than a desire to slake his thirst. And she left what she was saying unfinished as she swept her intrigued gaze away from him to seek out what held his concentrated attention.

"I ain't never been so dry that I've felt the need for a shot of liquor more than anything else, lady," he said in a forced monotone. "And if the feller who rode my horse to town is still in the cantina, a drink sure ain't going to be the first thing on my mind when I step inside."

"But you can't possibly know for sure that's your horse from this far away," Dinah asserted as she sat up on the trunk to get a better view of the town below.

"I'm sure," he said.

"But finding Pyle can't be that easy, Mr. Edge," the younger woman countered. "Whatever else he is, that swine isn't out and out stupid. Folks here must've told him Harry and me were headed back home after our business here. He surely wouldn't hang around town waiting for us to come after him."

"I know it's my horse is all, lady. If I need to make any guesses about anything else, it'll be later."

"Hush, baby," the redhead urged as she followed the half-breed's lead in looking at the buildings closer at hand.

The entire town was comprised of only fifty or sixty buildings, all of them single story and the majority of adobe construction. At the higher end of the street along which the wagon now rolled, both sides were lined with small, weather-ravaged houses. Some of them were quite obviously abandoned, while others, looking almost as derelict, had aromatic smoke spiraling from their chimneys. Several had piles of junk out back, and here and there a fence enclosed a yard, sometimes penning in a burro.

Twice the trio on the wagon heard babies wailing. One infant was being soothed by the soft singing of a woman. She sang a Mexican lullaby that for a moment stirred within Edge a long-forgotten memory of his father half humming and half singing the same song to Edge's younger brother on their Iowa farmstead.

"Wildwood is a crazy name for a town like this," Harriet Newton said, "but it seems there used to be some kind of petrified forest here a long time ago."

"And it was haunted," Dinah was quick to add. "That's the local Indian legend, anyway."

At the base of the slope, just above the desert flatland that extended to a line of rugged mountains in the distance, the street broadened into what passed for a plaza. The cantina, a derelict store with no name on its facade, and El Banco del Wildwood were sited on the west side, with the bank set at an angle to the widening street. Catty-corner to it was a church with a truncated tower, and immediately opposite the open-for-business drinking establishment was a stand of cottonwoods clumped in a patch of lush grass. A well was sunk into the ground nearby.

"Haunted forest of trees turned to stone, and a never-ending supply of sweet water," Harriet Newton said, taking up the history of the town again. "It was just too good for the Spanish priests from down south to let be. The Indians got chased out or killed, and the mission church got built." She shot a sharply quizzical look at Edge as he reined the team to a halt at the point where the street broadened into the plaza between the bank and the church. She kept talking in the same anxious whisper. "For a long time the holy men kept the place to themselves, praying all the while about how the Almighty had been so good to them by making the desert grow. Never did think to share their good luck with any poor people who hadn't taken the vows or whatever and—"

"This all happened a long time ago?" Edge asked evenly as he wound the reins around the brake lever.

"Oh, yes."

"It's what's not happening today that concerns me, lady."

With the wagon halted, the baby's wailing could be heard, carried down the hillside through the hot, smoke-tainted air of late afternoon. Then the sound was abruptly curtailed and there was just the low-keyed noise drifting out from the cantina to disturb the uneasy quiet of Wildwood.

"Things aren't usually this slow this time of day, huh?" Edge suggested.

"That's right, Mr. Edge," Dinah was quick to respond. Her gaze made another slow survey of the plaza and the street that twisted up the hill beyond the wagon. "There's always a few old-timers sitting in the shade under the trees. And children playing.''

The redhead cleared her throat to add, "And a lot of laughing that's plainly at us.''

"Which doesn't bother you," he reminded her of what she had said. He swung stiffly down to the ground with a grimace of pain that also held some irritation.

"We got used to that. Knew to expect it. But this . . .''

Harriet Newton cast apprehensive glances in all directions. She briefly took off the Army forage cap so she was better able to mop the sweat on her brow with a shirt-sleeve.

"If I had to guess, I'd say this town expects trouble, lady," the half-breed told her as he kept his glinting eyes directed toward the cantina. Inside, they heard talk intermingled with the clink of glass on glass and the chink of coins changing hands. Then he started away from the wagon.

"What are you doing?" the redhead demanded.

"You ain't armed!" the brunette called out fearfully.

"Going to see a man about a horse," the half-breed said flatly, not raising his voice. He was aware that what he was saying could carry easily into the cantina. "And if I have to guess again, I'd say it ain't the same man I aim to kill.''

They heard a soft barrage of gasps and shocked, quickly curtailed talk erupt from the cantina. Edge did not pause in his measured progress across the plaza, and in the silence each stride of his booted feet sounded disproportionately loud.

So too did the gunshot as a rifle bullet blasted out of the cantina and into the hard-packed surface of the plaza perhaps six inches away from the toe of Edge's leading foot. He froze and grimaced again. This time he was angry at himself for starting to move his right hand toward the empty holster. But his features were impassive again as he shifted the gaze of his slitted eyes up from the puff of dust that marked the bullet's point of impact in the ground. As he looked up he saw a man's head and shoulders above the batwing doors in the arched entrance of the cantina.

The smoke of the gunshot hung in the air for a second or so, partially veiling the face of the man who continued to aim the Winchester out over the tops of the batwings, gripping it in both hands, stock end hard to his shoulder and cheek pressed to the stock side, eye aligned behind the sights. But he had not pumped the lever action to eject the spent shellcase and jack a fresh bullet into the breech. Edge did not think the man had forgotten to do this.

One of the babies began to cry again, but the noise reached the plaza as a soft and unobtrusive sound. As Edge completed his next stride, he did not raise his voice, but still he was heard by the man in the cantina doorway some fifty feet away.

"You could've killed me with that first shot, feller."

"Easy as fallin' down and hittin' the ground."

"So why didn't you?"

The man was fat, not tall, and was about fifty years old. He had an unshaven face beneath a near bald head, and the grin of pride at his marksmanship was now replaced by perplexity.

"Huh?"

"Why didn't you kill me, feller?"

"Are you crazy or somethin'?" the fat man snarled. "You askin' to get your head shot off?" He shifted the aim of the rifle toward the center of the half-breed's chest. The barrel wavered wildly as he pumped the lever action of the repeater, but the muzzle was firmly fixed on the new target again before the expended case hit the hard-packed dirt in front of the cantina doorway. "If that's what you want, stranger, I can sure help you out!"

"We're looking for Delmar Pyle, Troy!" Harriet Newton yelled, her voice highly charged with emotion.

"He ain't here," Troy said, his glowering gaze at the half-breed as steady as the aim of the rifle. His voice started out hard, but became less so as he went on, "Don't think I won't plug you if that's the way it has to be, stranger."

"How will it have to be that way?" Edge asked, his voice icily calm and his gaze brutally hard as it bored into the sweat-beaded face of the fat man.

"If you lay a hand on that chestnut geldin' hitched to the post there."

"It's my horse."

"Pyle said you was a sore loser."

"He stole it off me."

"He said he won it in a game of chance. The saddle and gear too. And the Colt and Winchester. And money."

"He still have the guns?"

"Yeah. When he left town, that's all he had. We'd cleaned out the crazy fool. Everythin' he'd won off you except the pistol and rifle. Said he needed to keep those because he figured you'd come after him."

Edge looked briefly away from the cantina doorway and spat into the dust. And as he did so he saw that a number of men, women, and children had emerged from the houses on the slope. They stayed close to their homes, content to watch from a distance so they could duck back into safety should the even-toned talk on the plaza turn out to be a prelude to violence.

"He stole it all, and I aim to get it all back, feller."

Troy argued flatly, "It was won fair and square. The horse and what's on him by me. The money by Father Chevez."

"*Sí*, Señor Edge," a man confirmed from somewhere in the shade of the cantina behind Troy. "And there is no reason we should accept your word as the truth instead of that of Señor Pyle."

"Edge is right, priest!" Harriet Newton yelled, and the half-breed thought she sounded almost overconfident now. "That little creep didn't lie about Edge's name, but it seems like he told a pack of lies about the rest of it."

"How would you know?" Troy demanded. "You and your sweetheart was right here in town when Pyle and Edge was card playin'!"

Dinah McCall blurted, "And got back to our place to find the swine had wrecked it and messed it up and stole from Mr. Edge after cracking open his head with a shovel!"

Edge felt suddenly sick to his stomach and so tired he could not focus clearly. The anger he was nurturing toward Delmar Pyle had been burning slowly ever since he realized what the man had done to him. And now it was roaring, close to being out of control, as his desire to kill Pyle was forced down by the necessity to deal with these men.

For stretched seconds as the sun's bright yellow began to shade toward the dull crimson of short evening, he waited to see whether he would sink into quiet unconsciousness or let his anger explode into murderous rage. Or maybe neither would happen.

The man called Edge never gave in to anything if he could help it. And if he couldn't remain in control of this situation, if he couldn't come out on top in a fight with a couple of women, a small-town priest, and a fat slob of a cantina owner, then that son of a bitch Pyle would have done a lot more damage than just splitting open his head. He would have changed the man called Edge into somebody else.

"Hold it, mister!" Troy said.

"Edge, don't be crazy!" Harriet Newton cried out.

"Oh, my good Lord!" shrieked Dinah McCall.

"*Madre de Dios!*" Father Chevez said.

There was a burst of talk within the cantina and some calling back and forth among the watchers on the hillside. But the half-breed was able to hear clearly and identify his main protagonists as he continued to approach the arched entrance of the cantina, moving with slow deliberation, because that was the only way he could stay on his feet and walk in a straight line. He kept his glinting gaze fixed unwaveringly on the muzzle of Troy's Winchester.

"Another friggin' step and I'll blast you!" Troy said.

There was no longer any danger of an outbreak of rage from Edge. That would demand a greater degree of energy than he possessed right now. At least he had the brainpower left to realize that.

The Winchester blasted a second shot. He saw the spurt of smoke and stab of flame but knew he would not feel the pain of a bullet tearing into his flesh. For he had already seen the sharply in-focus muzzle suddenly drop from his chest.

Edge took another step, and another bullet dug into the dirt ahead of his slow-moving feet.

"You bastard!" the redhead cried.

"He ain't armed, Troy!" the brunette called.

"She's right, Marshall!" said the priest.

Then the repeater action was pumped and the muzzle was leveled at the vulnerable target once more as the shellcase spun through the air. Edge was just twenty feet away as the Winchester was jerked back behind the batwings. Troy's snarl of anger made it plain the move was not by his choice. Then his fat face and fleshy shoulders were gone from sight above the slatted doors and another man stood on the threshold. The flaps were pushed halfway open so that the newcomer was revealed from head to toe. He was a tall, emaciated man with a gaunt, sparsely bearded face above a grubby cleric's collar and a full-length cassock.

"Por favor, señor!" the priest entreated, and augmented the plea in his dark and sunken eyes by thrusting out his arms at full stretch, palms upturned and fingers splayed.

"You won my money, so I already gave," Edge rasped softly.

He approached the arched entrance of Marshall Troy's cantina, and the slatted batwings flapped emptily after the priest hurried to back out of his way, perhaps fearfully convinced Edge's rasping curses were directed exclusively at him. But the half-breed had been cursing at the entire world and everyone in it as part of his effort to keep his rage within bounds as he made his move on the cantina.

Edge's head throbbed and he was in the grip of a bone-deep weariness, but he was solidly on his feet and mentally alert as he thrust between the batwings, his elbows crashing them back against the walls.

He whirled to the left, sensing that the prime danger lurked in that direction. He had seen the Winchester and

Troy driven to that side of the entrance when Chevez stepped forcefully onto the threshold.

The fat man in the once white shirt, dark pants, and stained waist apron let out his pent-up breath with an inarticulate sound, given vicious meaning by the look in his blazing eyes. He sprang up from a half crouch and swung the rifle that he gripped with both hands around the barrel, aiming the stock toward the head of Edge.

Within the cantina, the whispering sound of the rifle broke the utter silence as it arced through the fetid air. Then Edge powered down into a crouch as the stock of the rifle crashed into the wall beside the arched entrance some twelve inches above the crown of the crouching man's Stetson. The man gripping the Winchester was forced by the momentum of the swing to turn to face Edge as the half-breed came upright even faster than he went down.

Edge took a step forward and brought one knee into vicious contact with the fat man's crotch. At the same time he landed a brutal punch into the fleshy belly that bulged above the tightly tied waist apron. Troy vented a split second of rage at missing his target with the clubbing blow. Then the snarl changed note to a scream of agony. He dropped the rifle and was forced to stumble backward by the punch. His hands reached for the source of the greater pain as he began to bend forward at the waist at the dictates of the lesser hurt. But then the same right fist that had knocked the wind out of him delivered a second punch. This time the blow was to the side of his fleshy and darkly stubbled jaw. It had enough power to whiplash him upright, turn him, and crash him back against the wall as his hands were snatched involuntarily from his crotch, his arms spread-eagled by the impetus of the sudden and violent change of direction.

Silence descended within the gloomy, malodorous, claustrophobic cantina again as Marshall Troy remained pressed to the adobe wall and teetered on the brink of oblivion. Edge stood in front and slightly to the side of the shorter man, clenching and unclenching the fist that hurt a little from the second punch. The half-breed could sense almost palpable waves of malevolence being directed at his back from an unknown number of eyes, and the volume of noise from outside the cantina quickly diminished, perhaps because the two women from the house in Dry River Valley came to a sudden halt at the arched entrance, refusing to enter after they had peered over the tops of the batwings.

The fat man conquered the threat of unconsciousness and for the first time in several seconds he was aware of his surroundings and his hurting and how these circumstances had come about. When this realization was complete, he scowled first at Edge's impassive face, then down at where one of the half-breed's booted feet rested hard on the frame of the discarded rifle. Next, as he moved his hands in to his body and gingerly explored his groin beneath the apron, his pained eyes sought and found another man to share in his hostility.

"Thanks for your help, Felipe," he rasped at the priest, then raked his reproachful gaze over the entire cantina before he spat out with even more enmity, "Thanks a whole friggin' lot. It's real good for a man to know he's got buddies like you, so that next time he'll know not to trust them any farther than he can see with his friggin' eyes shut!"

He stared down at the dirt floor as he finished condemning his patrons. Then he sent a stream of saliva onto the floor. Next he brought up his head to face Edge with an expression of defeat mixed with pain. His tone was dejected as he said, "Take the horse, since you feel so strong about it. But I won him in good faith in a fair and square game of chance."

"Ain't arguing with that, feller."

Perplexity gleamed through the dullness of pain in Troy's eyes as he growled, "So why'd you come on so strong, for frig sake?"

"Because he's crazy from that crack on the head that little creep gave him, I figure," Harriet Newton said sourly, through the doorway.

"And Mr. Edge don't like to have a gun aimed at him, Mr. Troy," the younger woman added.

"Especially when it's fired, feller," the half-breed added. "Usually try to warn people about that—when I'm carrying a gun of my own to back what I'm saying. Still ain't got one." He turned so that he could sweep his glittering, slit-eyed gaze over everyone in the cantina and in so doing shifted his foot off Troy's Winchester. "Anybody aims a gun at me better kill me with it, because I'll sure do my best to kill him. Or her."

The more than a dozen Mexicans who failed to hold Edge's gaze were aware of the tension crackling in the silence.

Marshall Troy challenged, "Ain't you never held a gun on a guy to keep him from doin' somethin', and not killed him if he did like you told him?"

"Sure, feller. But I made the rule, so I can be the exception that proves it."

Chevez put in apologetically, "Then the matter of the horse has not been resolved by this fight? So the money that I was *afortunado* enough to win for the church, that too need not be surrendered to you, Señor Edge?"

Edge pursed his lips, blew out a soft, whistling breath, and said, "I need God against me like I need a hole in the head, feller.'' He took off his hat and probed with gently exploring fingers the gash in his scalp at the top of his skull and murmured in a soured tone, ''One I've already got.''

''Where that swine Pyle hit him with a shovel,'' Dinah McCall reminded quickly.

''Wasn't just my name that Pyle told the truth about,'' the half-breed said as the fat Marshall Troy dragged a nearby chair away from a table and lowered himself gingerly, then gratefully down onto it. ''He also got it right about how I'm a sore loser.''

Chapter Five

WITH THE eruption of violence now uneasily calmed, the ill-dressed, unshaven, and sweatily unwashed patrons and owner of the evil-smelling cantina had the opportunity and the inclination to display their contempt for Harriet Newton and Dinah McCall, who continued to stand just outside the batwing doors. But, obviously in deference to the half-breed, who might be concealing a degree of regard for the couple behind his stone-faced attitude, no one voiced the usual taunts and insults. Until the redhead said icily, "Come on, Dinah. Mr. Edge, we're going to make a withdrawal from the bank, if you'll dicker prices for what you want here."

"Not from Luis Garcia's bank here in town you won't, sweethearts," Troy told them in a sneering tone as they started away from the cantina entrance.

Edge shifted his foot so that it rested on the rifle again.

"Why the hell not, for Pete's sake?" Dinah McCall demanded.

"Because Garcia left town today, that's why!"

"Shit!" Harriet Newton snarled.

Troy stretched back in the chair so he could peer out of a window. He gained confidence from the size of the throng as he challenged the half-breed, "If those sweet-hearts were real women, they sure as hell wouldn't be no ladies, huh?"

Edge had been rolling a cigarette as he took a longer look at the cantina and the men in it. He then checked the view outside that Troy had found so reassuring, and he ran the tip of his tongue along the cigarette paper; everything he did continued to mask the bad shape he was in. Beyond that surreptitious movement of his foot, he had managed not to react openly to the revelation the fat man had so enjoyed springing on the women.

"Was he traveling light or did he take his safe with him?"

"Nobody leaves this town with money that don't belong to them, mister." The fat man was still in pain, but his courage was being replenished by the moment. He looked out the window again before he added pointedly, "Nothin' that don't belong to them, if you get my drift."

With the exception of the priest, the men who had been drinking and playing cards in Troy's cantina all had the look of poverty-stricken peons. Their ages extending from thirty to more than fifty, they were raggedly dressed, unshaven, and unwashed for many days, and most of them had much the same undernourished look as Father Chevez. But it was not penny-ante poker they had been playing. The coins that Edge had first heard chinking as part of the general babble of the place were not just nickels and dimes being paid to Troy for shots of whiskey and tequila or glasses of beer. There were a number of silver dollars among the bills on the tables where one game of five-card draw and another of seven-card stud had been interrupted by the arrival of the wagon in town. And there were plenty of five and ten spots among the dollar bills and cartwheels in both pots. The Mexicans who looked as if they didn't have a peso among them kept casting nervous glances toward the money-littered tables. And nobody was more anxious about the display of wealth—and that it was apparently there for the taking by anyone willing to risk the consequences—than the priest.

The Winchester under the half-breed's right boot was the only weapon in plain sight within the dirty, overcrowded cantina.

Outside there were maybe two dozen people on the plaza between the cantina and the lush-growing stand of cottonwoods, most of them women. One—a Mexican— had a sleeping baby in her arms. Another was Chinese, and there were two Indians, a half-breed, and a pure white. They ranged from eighteen or even younger to maybe forty, and were as dirty and disheveled and underfed as the patrons of the cantina and the six men who stood outside with them in the failing light of the day. The six men—Edge realized there could be more beyond his angle of vision—differed from those inside the cantina in one obvious respect. Which was why Marshall Troy was feeling brave again. Each of them carried a rifle or a revolver.

"Garcia didn't say nothing to us this morning about leaving town!" Harriet Newton protested as she returned to the threshold of the cantina and peered inside.

"Surely there's some way we can get our money?" the younger woman implored, and although Edge could not see her, he could visualize her plumply pretty face turning this way and that.

Troy taunted, "I guess Luis didn't tell you about his business across the border because he figured it wasn't none of your business to know it, sweethearts!"

"But you *mujerio* know how you can make much *dinero*, eh?" one of the Mexican women on the plaza suggested sardonically, and concluded the innuendo with a spit.

The fat man who still massaged his injured genitals beneath the apron leaned back in his chair again to survey the scene on the plaza. He did this as several other women vented short bursts of cynical laughter.

"Hey, that's how we can work this thing out, Edge!" Troy announced with high enthusiasm as the half-breed struck a match on the wall to light his cigarette. "You know the setup in this town."

"It's coming to me, feller."

"The sweethearts didn't tell you?"

The half-breed's fast glance at the redhead on the threshold was not lost on her. She started to explain, "I was getting around to it, wasn't I? But the whole thing just disgusts me so much I—"

"You think what you and your sweetheart get up to together ain't disgustin' to normal people?" Troy cut in on her. He seemed to be gripped by a mood of genuine revulsion as he glowered at her, even to the extent of snatching his hand from under the apron as if he was anxious that nobody should think his massaging his groin had a sexual motive while he was talking to the woman at the doorway. Then he spat at the floor to further impress upon those who could see him that he was revolted by the women from Dry River Valley. He shifted his scowling gaze to Edge and altered the shape of his expression to convey eagerness again as he went on quickly, "It don't look like it yet, mister, but Wildwood is gonna get to be a wide open, rip-roarin' border town. Gonna get to be the best place in the whole of the territories and the whole of the country of Mexico for a man to come visit if it's whorin' or gamblin' or such he wants. You seen the cash on the card tables here. And so far we just been gettin' small-potato business from the Federale post at San Sarita and the claim stakers out of Hopeville. Why, when the word gets spread, we're gonna be richer—"

"I ain't looking to get rich, feller," Edge cut in. He saw that all but one of Marshall Troy's patrons were allowing themselves to get caught up in the excitement generated by the fat man. Only the priest did not nod and grin and lick his lips in anticipation of the future that was being predicted for the wretched citizens of this squalid town on a borderland hillside. "Just to get back what was stolen from me," Edge explained.

The fat man scowled again, but then he shrugged and with a lot less enthusiasm he said, "So, okay. Town like this could use a guy like you. And it's a cryin' shame about the sweethearts. Way we're so short on the pure white stuff. But what d'you say to a small game of chance, Mr. Edge?"

"What kind of evil are you cooking up in that filthy mind of yours now, Troy?" the redhead demanded bitterly.

"Any game you choose that can be played with a deck of cards," Troy went on, ignoring the angry woman at the doorway who had a hand hooked over one of the batwings. "We ain't got any roulette or crap tables or wheel of fortune or stuff like that yet. Just you and me, what d'you say? For your horse and gear? And if you win them, I'll stake some cash. Enough so you can buy a couple of weapons, in case you need a gun before you catch up with Pyle and get back your own.''

"I guess you don't take markers, feller.''

A crooked smile slid across the fat man's sweaty face and he nodded. "Strictest rule we got in town.'' He laughed. "About the only rule. No markers. But a guy in your position don't need no credit, does he?'' He jerked a thumb. "Maybe they ain't like real women in lotsa ways, Edge, but they got what's essential for a woman to—''

"You make me feel sick to my stomach, you son of a—''

"Marshall, this is *estúpido*!'' the priest interrupted the woman's snarled attack. His tone was almost as hard as that of the redhead.

"Harry?'' Dinah McCall implored, sounding like a frightened child.

"Someone named Harry is supposed to have balls and a pecker, sweetheart!'' the fat man mocked.

Edge didn't feel he had rested enough in the wake of the brief beating he had given Marshall Troy, but he was still able to go smoothly down on his haunches, snatch at the Winchester, move his foot off it, and come powering upright again. He turned as he did all this and put his back to the adobe wall between the doorway and the window. He could not recall if Troy had pumped the lever action of the repeater after firing the last shot, so he pumped it now and didn't care whether the ejected shell was a live one or an empty case.

The burst of noise that had exploded from many throats as he made his move abruptly ended as he angled the Winchester from his hip toward the area of the fat man's waist apron that covered his genitals.

Edge said flatly, "You sound like a feller who doesn't like trouble, Father Chevez."

The noise inside the cantina had indicated to those outside that something was wrong. In the street the armed men and a few of the women started suddenly forward. The men demanded to know what was happening.

"Stay back!" the priest roared in near panic as he swung to the doorway as the redhead backed away from him. With the batwings thrust half open again, he was in full view of everyone on the plaza in the fading light. No one was left in any doubt about his earnestness as he gestured frantically with both arms. "Marshall will be killed if you come closer!"

The advance was halted, and some people even began to back off.

"If not killed, maybe something even worse?" Edge growled, constantly flicking his gaze between the terrified face of Troy and the muzzle of the Winchester. The man's sweating, bristled flesh kept trembling in spasms, and Edge felt there was a danger he might get the shakes himself, but the rifle barrel remained steady.

"First and foremost I am a man of God, Señor Edge," Father Chevez supplied in response to the half-breed's comment. His voice sounded almost serene in contrast to the tone he had used to hold off those outside the cantina. "To go in peace and to have all about me go in peace is a large part of my life's work."

"Señor, you want we should light a lamp?" one of the Mexicans at the rear of the small place asked tentatively.

The half-breed let a breath rasp out through clenched teeth. Edge was relieved that it was getting dark.

"No, feller. Maybe save the match to light a candle for this feller. Later."

His slitted eyes remained fixed in a cold stare at the quaking Troy. Then he felt confident enough in his command of the situation to glance toward the priest. In the soft light of the setting sun he saw for the first time that Felipe Chevez was probably not yet thirty years of age, that his insubstantial beard and the pocked gauntness of his features made him seem much older.

"Hey, Edge," Marshall Troy said tremulously. He even tried to grin. "I was only gonna make the suggestion we play some kinda strip poker, you know? Just for laughs. No harm intended. Just to see if them women from out in the valley really got—"

"It is best if you keep quiet, I think, Marshall," Chevez advised as the fat man found himself unable to continue speaking in the face of Edge's glittering gaze and the rock-steady aim of the rifle at his crotch.

"Edge, is there anything you want from Dinah and me?" Harriet Newton called anxiously.

"Some quiet would be nice, lady."

His irony drew a snarl from the redhead. Then the priest hurried to pick up the threads of his exchange with the half-breed:

"Mostly there is peace of a kind in this town, señor." He shook his head slowly and a morose frown spread across his face as he said, "Not peace of mind for certain of us, but God's world will never be perfect while men walk through it. And to do God's work, some of his disciples must make a compromise. The money that I am able to raise here in Wildwood, which was once a holy place, will be put to spiritual good in other places where—"

"Goddammit, Felipe!" the distraught Troy cut in tautly. "I'm in real trouble here, and there ain't never been a time I wanted less to hear a Holy Joe givin' a friggin' sermon."

The fat man's gaze constantly shifted back and forth between Edge and Chevez. He blinked a great deal and kept darting his tongue between his lips while he made the plea.

"You and me have some common ground, feller," the half-breed told him.

"Look, just take your horse and be on your way, mister. That rifle likewise." He leaned back in the chair to look and shout through the window, "Strangers are gonna leave now, you people! You go on home and let them take off without no trouble, you hear!"

His back to the wall, with no view of the plaza, Edge heard some soft-toned talk and the shuffling sounds of feet. Marshall Troy nodded in satisfaction.

Dinah McCall called excitedly, "Mr. Edge, they're doing like he told them."

"*Bueno*, Señor Edge," Chevez allowed dolefully. "You and Marshall are right. This is hardly the moment for me to explain how I consider certain ends justify the means. You have brought trouble to Wildwood where there is almost always peace. When there is not peace, Marshall has always been able to deal with the trouble."

"That's my given name, mister," Troy put in, his tone and expression falsely bright as he strove to draw some of the high tension out of the atmosphere. "Marshall, same as some lawmen are called. And I sometimes need to act like a kinda lawman when there's trouble needs dealin' with."

"I think that this trouble does not need dealing with, perhaps?" Chevez queried Edge. "It will just go away?"

"With my horse and gear and this rifle," the half-breed answered, hoping that in the gloomy light of the cantina the effort needed to keep his voice even was not seen by anyone.

"It's all clear out here now," Harriet Newton reported.

"I told you—take what you want," Troy urged.

There were some rapid-fire comments from several of Troy's customers, all speaking in their native language and variously warning of dire consequences if Edge should attempt to take any of the money off the tables and scorning the fat man for repudiating what he had said earlier about nobody leaving Wildwood with anything that did not belong to him.

"I'm half Mexican and understand the entire language," Edge said in American to stem the talk and check what the priest had it in mind to say. Then he gestured with his head and told Troy, "On your feet, feller."

The fat man swallowed hard and demanded, "What for?" But he rose from the chair, his trepidation over what the future might hold numbing the effects of the recent painful past.

"I'm going to back up to the doorway, feller. The priest is going to step out ahead of me, and you'll leave right after me."

"Best to do as he tells us, I think," Chevez advised anxiously.

He pushed open the batwings and Edge moved sideways along the wall. The fat man took short steps to match the half-breed's sluggish pace and said tautly, "I'm the one with a gun aimed at a mighty unfortunate place, Felipe. I ain't about not to do like I'm told." He waited until all three of them were out on the plaza with the two women from Dry River Valley before he added, "Long as he don't want the friggin' impossible."

The atmosphere felt a great deal cooler outside the malodorous cantina. A three-quarter moon hung low in a cloudless sky, and in its blue-tinged light he saw clearly that the two women had not stood idly and helplessly by since he announced in the cantina that he intended to leave town. Dinah McCall was up on the wagon seat, the reins in one hand and the Winchester in the other, and Harriet Newton stood beside the gelding, her Remington drawn while her free hand rested on the post to which the horse was hitched. Up on the slope where the street wound above them, all was quiet except for sporadic sobbing of one of the fretful babies. Here and there a window or doorway spilled the light of a candle or kerosene lamp. The smell of woodsmoke and cooking chili was less pungent now, as the fires had been allowed to dwindle.

"What now?" the redhead asked, still nurturing her ill feeling toward the half-breed for scorning her offer of help.

"You ride on the wagon and I'll take my horse," he told her.

She spat into the dust and jammed the forage cap more firmly on her head as she turned on her heels and strode toward the flatbed and pair.

Without being told to, the priest had moved to stand alongside Troy just outside the cantina entrance.

"Please go in peace, and I wish you well in your endeavors to—"

"That's pulpit talkin' you're doin' again, Felipe," Marshall Troy cut in sourly. Like Edge, the fat man seemed to feel easier and more in control of himself out in the cool, clear air of evening. "Don't mean nothin' unless them that are hearin' it go along with your kinda thinkin'." He spoke more quickly and powered the words with a greater degree of contempt as Edge backed away toward the post where the horse was hitched.

Harriet Newton had already climbed up on the wagon and confiscated the reins from the younger woman.

Edge went around to the left side of the gelding, unhitching the reins from the post as he did so.

"You ladies didn't lie to me about having money in the bank here in town?" he called across the plaza, driving the fat man into intrigued silence.

"Of course not!" Dinah McCall replied indignantly.

"At least a hundred bucks?" the half-breed suggested as he swung up into the saddle. He felt dizzy and noticed Troy looking toward the wagon.

"That's none of your business!" the redhead snapped.

The other woman on the wagon seat started to say something in a whispering tone of complaint, but was shushed into irate silence.

"A hundred bucks is what I'm prepared to pay for what you said I could have, feller," Edge told Troy to recapture the fat man's increasingly interested attention. "These ladies give you permission to withdraw that much from what they've got in Garcia's bank. Figure enough people are hearing this so the banker will be sure it's a straight deal."

"If the *mujerio* will tell me they authorize such a transaction," Troy said, "Luis Garcia will accept my word that it is—"

"Shit, a hundred it is!" Harriet Newton snarled, and thrust her revolver in its holster so she could take a two-handed grip on the reins.

Dinah McCall vented a small squeal of delight that conveyed her relief they were at last on the point of leaving Wildwood.

"It's daylight robbery, but I ain't in no position to haggle, looks like," the fat man growled as Edge canted the rifle to his shoulder and struck a match on the side of the stock to relight the cigarette that had hung unsmoked from a corner of his mouth for so long. Then he took up the reins and tugged on them to make the horse turn away from the post.

"*Aquí, hombre!*" a man in the cantina said in a rasping whisper. A half second later Edge would not have heard the voice and recognized its quality of tense urgency against the thud of hooves and clatter of turning wheels as the redhead started the wagon rolling.

But he had already halted the turn of his mount and begun to bring the rifle down from his shoulder, his head wrenched around to the side, before Chevez snarled, "*Esta loco!*"

For part of a second Marshall Troy teetered on the brink of agreeing that it was a crazy play. But whatever degree of respect he commanded in this town was based upon his unofficial status as peace officer. Already he had been cruelly humiliated, but he could have lived with that if one of his fellow citizens had not pushed a revolver toward him above the batwing doors, butt first with the hammer already thumbed back.

Such an opportunity to strike back at the arrogant stranger who had hurt him so badly could not be turned down. Especially since he would be striking back the best way there was.

The fraction of time was gone and the smile on the fat man's face that had been only half formed suddenly became a beaming grin of premature triumph. This, as his pudgy hand closed in a fist on the butt of the revolver, his index finger curled around the trigger.

He spun from the waist, thrusting out the gun to the limit of his reach as a chorus of voices was raised in the cantina. At the same time, Dinah shrieked a warning, Harriet hauled on the reins to bring the wagon to an abrupt halt, and the two horses in the traces snorted their ill temper at the countercommand.

Edge whipped the rifle down from his left shoulder and squeezed the trigger of the Winchester at the instant the barrel came to rest in the angle of his bent right elbow. He blasted a bullet into the center of Marshall Troy's right cheek over a range of perhaps fifteen feet; this gave the damaging bullet enough velocity to pass through the head of the fat man and explode out of the nape of his neck in a spraying welter of gore and bone fragments.

A spasm of a dying muscle pressed Troy's finger to the trigger of his revolver as he was sent staggering backward on legs that ceased to function. As he thudded against one of the batwings, his shot cracked into the hard-packed dirt of the plaza and the gun from which it was fired dropped free of his lifeless fingers. The doors flapped open and Troy slumped dead across the threshold of his cantina.

Chevez made the sign of the cross and exclaimed in shock, *"Por Dios!"*

Edge worked the lever action of the rifle and snarled, "Any other high roller ready to cash in his chips?"

The priest recovered instantly from the horror of the sudden killing and whirled to grip the tops of the batwings and rasp a command to everyone inside that they should hold still. His order silenced the sudden swell of talk.

"Just go," the priest said flatly.

"You heard the man, ladies," Edge called across the plaza, his tone as cold as that of Chevez.

There was a brief exchange of anxious whispers between Harriet and Dinah, then the redhead flicked the reins and snapped a command that set the wagon rolling again. The half-breed remained in the half turn astride his horse, the cocked Winchester aimed in the general direction of the cantina entrance where Felipe Chevez stood, his gaunt face impassive.

"*Hasta la vista, señor,*" the priest said pointedly after the wagon had been driven far enough off the plaza so the clattering sounds of its progress didn't interfere with his words.

"And do not come back, *asesino*!" a man roared from inside the cantina.

Chevez snapped his head to the side to direct a stream of low but venomous Mexican over the top of the batwings. Edge heard only an occasional word clearly but from it was able to decipher that the priest was counteraccusing the man inside of killing Marshall Troy by passing him the pistol. The half-breed eased forward the hammer of the Winchester and slid the rifle into the forward hung boot when Chevez finished with his recriminations against the men in the cantina.

He continued explaining in louder American, "I tell them that he is dead because he was a fool and they will be *loco* for the rest of their lives if they do not learn to accept defeat when victory is impossible. And against a man like you, señor—a *pistolero*—Marshall Troy had not the chance of a snowflake in the desert."

"He was a gambling man who figured the odds wrong and lost, feller," Edge responded unconcernedly as he heeled his mount forward. But he continued to look back at the cassock-garbed man outside the batwing doors as a lamp was lit and pale light shafted from the entrance and windows of the cantina. "And every gambler knows, when you're hot you're hot; when you're not, you're not."

"*Como?*" Chevez asked across the widening distance.

Edge knew then that he had not imagined he was talking like a man filled with liquor—he really was slurring his words. He ended his backward gaze at the priest to face front and peer toward the wagon, which was halted out on the trail that cut across the desert to the south. But although the women were waiting for him, he was not certain he could stay in the saddle long enough to reach them. He was in no condition to estimate distances nor was there any need to. He could see the wagon and the women on the seat clearly in the bright moonlight, and as long as this remained so, he could stay up on the chestnut gelding and keep the horse heading in the right direction. But if once he allowed his vision to be fuzzed by the same aberration that had got to his vocal cords, then he was finished. He would pass out and topple to the ground like a helpless drunk.

He sure could use a drink—tequila with a whole mess of salt—to replenish what had been lost in sweat. Then, so suddenly it almost shocked him into unconsciousness, he came level with the front of the wagon. He reined in his mount and discovered it was even more of an effort to stay astride the unmoving animal.

"You took your damn time, mister!" the redhead growled.

"For Pete's sake, Harry, the man is sick!" the younger woman said quickly and anxiously as she clambered down off the wagon. "He looks . . . he looks like death."

"You win, lady," he said, making a conscious effort to speak distinctly.

"Win?" Dinah McCall murmured, confused. "Harry, what the—"

"Hot I'm not anymore."

"Shit, the guy's delirious!" Harriet snarled, directing

a worried glance back toward Wildwood as she scrambled down off the wagon.

"Death warmed up, is all," Edge murmured, no longer caring how he sounded or if what he said could be understood. He had got to the wagon, and that was all that mattered to him.

"If the people back there spot how sick you are, mister," the redhead rasped with a jerk of a thumb toward town, "we could all of us wind up stone-cold dead as Troy."

"Oh, my good Lord!" Dinah said with a kind of gasping shrillness after she had shot a glance back along the trail and seen the throng gathering on the plaza. Then she tugged at the half-breed's forearm as she pleaded, "Please, Mr. Edge. Don't allow your brains to get all scrambled up now. Not when we need you to help us."

"That's one thing we can be sure of, baby," Harriet interrupted sourly, glowering up into the sweat-beaded, haggard face of the tall man astride the gelding. "He can't be suffering from no brain damage, because men like him don't have any brains."

Edge allowed himself to be guided rather than helped from the saddle by the worried brunette. Then, making another enervating effort to be coherent, he said evenly, "You won the first game, lady." He stabbed a forefinger toward the still-scowling redhead as he added, "With her, there's no contest."

"Please," Dinah begged.

"Like I say, delirious, baby," Harriet said.

"On account of I don't get into a battle of wits with someone who ain't armed."

Chapter Six

EDGE AWOKE the following morning with a feeling of nausea accompanying the pounding ache inside his skull. But by forcing himself to remain on his back beneath the blankets, slitted eyes gazing into the incomplete darkness of his Stetson, he made the threat of throwing up subside. When this danger of humiliating himself in front of the two women had been beaten, he started to work on the pain in his head. Soon the pain's assault reverberated down the scale until it became bearable and he was able to think lucidly about what was happening to him.

In a moment his thoughts were interrupted as he listened to Harriet Newton and Dinah McCall preparing breakfast. And, he noticed gratefully, the air was warm, not hot.

He already had a reasonably fair impression of the place where the night camp had been made. Now he gulped two or three breaths of morning air and demanded, ''You say anything that needs an answer?''

The redhead with the plainer but more sensuous face replied, "I said good morning, hard man. But I reckon you ain't so sure about that."

The fuller-bodied, conventionally pretty younger woman showed the other a reproachful frown, then eyed Edge with a mixture of concern and pity as she said, "Harry can be real cruel sometimes, mister. But don't you pay her no mind right now. I was asking how you felt and if you were feeling well enough to have some of this beef and beans and grits I've cooked up."

"It's a better morning than it was a night," Edge replied as he rose gingerly to his feet, the top blanket falling down from his fully clothed body. To the other he answered, "Coffee'll maybe give me an appetite for the food."

"Hope so, Mr. Edge. Food's the best cure for illness, my ma used to say. And I reckon you're the same as Harry and me—didn't have a thing to eat all day yesterday, huh?"

She poured him strong coffee in his own tin cup and he signaled for her to stay by the fire with the redhead as he reached to take the cup.

"Obliged."

"You're welcome."

"Son of a bitch," he commented good-humoredly, "it's like being at a church picnic."

The campsite was brightly lit by the new day's sun, and it looked much as the half-breed recalled it from his brief survey during his short moments of clear thinking the previous night. It was in a fold between two barren, low hills. The bottomland of the shallow draw they were in was thickly layered with gritty dust and heavily littered with sharply angled fragments of rock. The women had collected some of the larger rocks to form a circle in which they had built a fire of limbs torn off the stunted mesquite that grew in widely scattered thickets on the flanking slopes. The fire now burned evenly under the skillet and coffee pots, sending up a column of smoke that would be visible to anyone who was looking out across the desert from Wildwood. In the clear air of early morning, the adobe buildings on the plaza and along the town's winding single street were clearly visible from the camp.

The trail that left the plaza at the foot of the distant hill cut a straight line across the desert, came up through the draw, and then curved out of sight as it completed a first step up through the rising country of the Sierra Madre foothills. The camp had been pitched just off the trail.

After the two women had watched with different degrees of interest while Edge made a cursory study of their surroundings, Dinah McCall scolded the older woman.

"Ain't no reason, Harry, seems to me, why people can't talk civil to each other, no matter where they are. Don't you think that, mister?"

Edge rasped the back of a brown-skinned hand along the thick bristles on his jaw and answered, "Unless I have to, I try not to take sides in domestic disagreements. The Wildwood banker—Garcia—don't ride horseback?"

"I was just—"

"A buckboard," Harriet Newton cut in flatly. "You really are an expert at reading sign, ain't you?"

"Anyone would have to be blind not to see that two four-wheeled rigs came down this trail recently, lady," the half-breed answered. "The one you parked here and another that went on up the draw."

The coffee had cooled enough so that he was able to

half swallow some of it without scalding his throat. Its strength killed the taint of nauseous bile in his mouth and left him with just the nagging ache in his head. On the beneficial side, he felt well rested, and with the last vestige of nausea neutralized, the smell of the cooking food began to make him hungry.

"Easy to see in the light of day," Harriet said in the same monotone as before while she attended to the meat and grits frying in the skillet and the beans simmering in the pot.

"For Pete's sake!" Dinah snapped, coming suddenly upright after filling two more cups with coffee. She whirled to take them toward a patch of shade at the side of the wagon, where the heavy trunk had been offloaded. Its top had been spread with a cover on which were three cramped place settings. "We all want the same thing! To see that swine Pyle pays for what he done to us! And we all agreed to stay together until it's been done! There ain't no reason in the world, far as I can see, why any of us has to bicker with the others over anything!"

Edge took more than passing notice of them for the first time since he had woken up, and saw that they were dressed the same as yesterday. But whereas the slender redhead had apparently done no more than wash her hands and face to remove the sweat and grime of the trail, the younger woman had taken more trouble to look her best. Her long, black, naturally curled hair was neat and sheened from a vigorous brushing, and she had got most of the loose dust off her hat and clothes. Her boots looked to have been buffed by more than a mere wipe, and most obvious of all, she had hitched in her belt by another notch, which had the effect of emphasizing the narrowness of her waist above her flared hips and tightly gripped her shirt so that the tautness of the stretched fabric clearly showed the contours of her full breasts and the nipples that topped them.

"I don't see anything to fight over either," Edge agreed after looking long and hard at the pretty brunette over the rim of the cup while he sipped at the coffee. But when she turned from stooping over the improvised table, she found he was now directing his entire attention at her partner, who endeavored to appear anything but desirably feminine. Dinah's half-formed smile of pleasure at the man's agreement suddenly had a frozen quality as she saw something in his bristled and dirty profile that signaled his double meaning. Which, she was also quick to spot, was not lost on Harriet, who even gave a small nod of acknowledgment. In a moment the half-breed added, "But I might just start to get a little riled unless some straight talking gets done."

The redhead was abruptly hard-eyed and tight-lipped again after she had seemed on the point of unbending from her severe attitude after Edge's comment that he had no sexual designs on Dinah. She said, "Let's eat" as if this was her final comment.

Sullen in a childlike way again, Dinah brought the three tin plates from the table and asked grudgingly, "You want some of the grub, mister?"

"Coffee did the trick with my gastric juices."

"So sit," Harriet instructed as he came to the fire and held out his plate.

He refilled his cup from the coffee pot, and one of them took his plate, heaped high with the good-smelling food, to the makeshift table. While both women sat cross-legged on the ground to eat, he elected to drag his saddle out from under the wagon where it had been stowed and sit on it rather than in the dirt.

Only the sounds of eating disturbed the otherwise perfect silence of the morning. The meal didn't take long, since they were all ravenously hungry. But after a minute more of silence as they sipped their coffee, the women began to talk. The brunette spoke first, grimacing at Edge, who had taken out his makings.

"You smoke too much, you know that?" she rebuked him mildly, obviously just for something to say.

"It's the only vice I have, lady," he replied evenly. "When there's no available woman or liquor around."

The grimace expanded to a scowl, and she looked set to snarl a retort but could not call to mind an appropriate insult and so pushed herself to her feet with an indignant grunt.

"You don't count it a vice that you kill people as easy as others would step on a bug?" Harriet asked as Dinah gathered up the dirty plates and cutlery and swaggered toward the fire, swaying her hips as she went.

"Kind of people I kill, lady," Edge told her as he lit the cigarette with a match struck on the nearest wagon wheel, "it's the same as stepping on bugs."

There was another, shorter period in which nobody spoke. Dinah busied herself with cleaning off the dirty dishes and cooking utensils with the gritty dust, and Harriet and the half-breed remained on opposite sides of the covered trunk. He smoked and gazed into the middle distance where heat haze now obscured the town on the hill slope across the desert and was aware that he needed to wince less frequently now as the pain between his eyes seldom stabbed him with any sharpness. He was also aware that the redhead with the sensuous looks and the firm, slender body often raised her thoughtful green eyes from the contents of her cup to glance at him.

"Headache not so bad now?" she asked at length.

"The one Delmar Pyle gave me with the shovel?"

She nodded.

"What's he talking about, Harry?" the brunette wanted to know, interrupting the chore of kicking dirt onto the fire.

"I think, baby, that we're a headache that ain't so easy to shake off," she answered, but an arching of her eyebrows under the peak of the forage cap also made it serve as a query to Edge.

"We made a deal," he said, dumping the dregs from his cup and then cleaning it out himself. "The fact that Troy's dead is neither here nor there. I'm into you ladies for the hundred dollars I promised to pay for the horse and the rest of the stuff. Then, last night, you took care of me when I was in no condition to look out for myself. Got me clear of that town where I was likely to get lynched without knowing what the hell was going on. And then you got me out to here where you bedded me down and let me sleep long and easy. Won't shake you off by my choice until I'm clear of those debts you're owed."

"By killing that swine Pyle," Dinah snarled venomously as she brought the cleaned pots and dishes toward the wagon. Her ill humor with Edge was now completely gone as she recalled how much more cause she had to feel enmity toward the other. "And he's the worst kinda creeping, crawling, slipping, and sliding bug there is, that's my opinion."

Harriet waited patiently for the younger woman to bring the tirade to an end and just glanced at her in the manner of an indulgent and long-suffering parent who has come to terms with a headstrong offspring.

Edge had already stowed his cup. Now he took the

plate and knife and spoon proffered by Dinah and put them in a saddlebag. While he did this, he was aware that the brunette no longer made any deliberate effort to flaunt the obvious sexuality of her body, though with such a body still blatantly delineated by the manner in which she wore the masculine garb, every jounce of her breasts, turn of her waist, and sway of her hips was plain to see. He was equally aware that Harriet could see the same display and had one eye on him, alert for the slightest prurient reaction. And not until she was certain that his impassiveness was a true reflection of how he felt about the younger and prettier woman did she suggest with a deep sigh, "Why not let's finish up here and get rolling, mister? Better than sitting around here wasting time while I tell you the whole thing."

"I'll go along with that," Dinah agreed eagerly.

Edge rose to his feet and hefted the saddle up off the ground. He drawled, "Let's hope this is the kind of story that has a happy ending."

Chapter Seven

HARRIET NEWTON said in a tentative tone of voice as soon as she had flicked the reins and geed the wagon team forward, "Dinah and me have plans to get into the horse-trading business up in Dry River Valley, Edge. It's something we both want to do, and once we get the operation running smooth and easy, there won't be no need for us to fret about what other folks think of the way we are."

Dinah McCall sat up on the seat beside the redhead and hooked a reassuring hand over her shoulder. The half-breed rode the gelding to the left of the wagon, level with the seat, drawing against the cigarette angled from his lips just often enough to keep it from going out. All the time, he kept his customary watch over the terrain in all directions, his attitude suggesting, incorrectly, that he was paying only scant attention to what the woman was saying.

"We first got the idea of horse ranching when we

85

lived in New York City. But we didn't know anything about it, that's for sure. We just wanted to get away from people. People that couldn't understand about the way Dinah and me are. And because they couldn't see how it was for us, they didn't like us or was kinda scared of us. Made life hell for us wherever we lived. Wherever we went.''

''We got spat at, had rocks tossed through our house windows, folks sent us mail filled with all kinds of language that made out we done all kinds of things we never and—''

''Let me tell it, baby,'' the older woman cut in, her tone calm in contrast to Dinah's shrill excitement at remembered outrages. Dinah withdrew her hand from the shoulder of Harriet, who was now firmly in control of herself as she took up the story. ''Like I said, they made life unbearable for us in New York and I guess we knew in our hearts that it wouldn't be much better when we came out west. Because country people can be worse bigots than them in the city when it comes to what they don't figure is right and clean and wholesome and natural. But we figured there was space out here anyway. Plenty of it, where we might be able to live the way we wanted a long way from the sons of . . .''

Her grip on herself was not as strong as it had seemed, and Edge thought that the redhead probably nursed a more bitter and deeply entrenched resentment against the world than did the younger woman, who flared up to anger very fast but just as quickly forgot again what had touched off the fuse.

''You planned a horse ranch in Dry River Valley?'' he asked as Harriet, tight-lipped and dull-eyed, fought to suppress the rage at a thousand and one past injustices.

She took a few moments more to regain her composure,

but she had not been so immersed in bitter memories that she failed to hear clearly what Edge said. She shot a hard glance at him, as if she expected to see an expression of implied criticism that had not sounded in his voice. She found he was his usual impassive self.

"We soon gave up the ranching idea when we got out here to the territories, Mr. Edge," she told him tautly. "We have some money, but not enough to start anything on a big scale. Then, we heard there was business to be had out of bringing horses up from Mexico to sell north of the border. And that's what we plan to do from the place in the valley."

"*Planned* to do anyways," Dinah said sourly as she emerged from a reverie to cast a baleful glance about her at the rugged wilderness on all sides.

"Baby, baby," Harriet soothed, and it was her turn to offer reassurance with a hand on the other woman's arm. "If you and me can't bounce back after we been knocked over with the lousy end of the stick, who can? We sure have had enough practice, ain't we?"

"For Pete's sake, Harry, that's damn right!" Dinah answered, shrugging off despair as easily as she had anger.

"Pyle only made a mess of your place," Edge said pointedly. "He didn't burn it down. And Mexico's still full of mustangs."

The older woman nodded curtly as she returned her hand to the reins, her thin face expressing determination.

"We were doing fine. Found the old shack, and it was big enough to hold all the stuff we'd brought from the city to make us feel at home. And Luis Garcia put us in touch with some *vaqueros* out of San Sarita who were willing to round up and bring us the wild horses."

"Trouble was, he put Delmar Pyle in touch with us

too," Dinah McCall put in, but with no emotion in her voice. She merely felt the need to contribute to the account.

"For which we thanked our lucky stars at the time," the redhead went on and drew a grudging nod of agreement from the brunette. "There was plenty of heavy work to do, fixing up the shack that no one had lived in for ten years or so and fencing off a corral, then digging the well. Pyle did it all with a will, and he did it for little enough plus his board and a place to bed down at the side of the shack. And the wages we did pay him we didn't give him in cash. Way Pyle wanted it done, Luis Garcia took money out of our deposit each week and put it in his. That way he had no ready cash to gamble with. Gambling was his downfall was how he told it. Reason he went to Wildwood in the first place—he'd heard it was for men looking for easy money in games of chance. And easy women.

"But the women didn't interest him, he said." She spat at the drawpole between the swaying rumps of the team in the traces. The gesture served to defuse her anger. "Lost every cent he had in card games in Troy's cantina. He was in a real sad state before Garcia got him the job at our place."

Although the trail was now running through bare mountain terrain, only the distant peaks to the south and west reared toward spectacular altitudes. In the north and the east, the rock ridges were never more than a hundred feet or so high, letting the morning sun glare down on the wagon and its lone escort with intensifying ferocity as the day progressed. Only infrequently, when they rode close along the base of a short escarpment or a pillar of rock were the two women and the man able to briefly relish a notion of coolness.

"It sure is hot," Dinah complained. She pulled the front of her shirt away from her sweaty flesh and blew a breath of air into the cleft between her breasts.

"I wish you wouldn't keep butting in, baby," the redhead chided as the younger woman took off her Stetson to use as a fan as she mopped at her pretty face with a kerchief.

"For Pete's sake, you don't have to be so touchy, Harry!"

Edge didn't think it was the heat that was causing Harriet Newton's ill humor, nor the guilelessly provocative actions of Dinah McCall which the half-breed might have seen as tantalizing.

"You've told me enough so that I can make a good guess at what you're scared to tell me, lady," he said, and sensed both of them looking hard at him as he took a slow drink from one of his canteens.

"You ain't as smart as you think you are, mister!" the redhead claimed as he restoppered the canteen and hung it back over the saddlehorn. "I ain't afraid to tell you a damn thing! It's just that I don't like having to admit I've been played for a sucker. That's what's getting me tongue-tied all the time."

"Happens to the best of us from time to time, lady."

"You really are an arrogant bast—"

"*Us* includes a whole lot of people in a big world," he cut in as he arced away his cigarette butt.

They passed a slab of two-by-four rock off the trail to the right. Shaped and upended by natural forces, it resembled a tombstone, but the painted lettering on each side, faded by long exposure to the elements, did not proclaim a last resting place. On the north-facing side was painted BORDER and on the opposite side FRONTERA.

The women gave no sign that they were aware of leaving one country to enter another, and for several seconds there was only the clop of hooves and the sounds of the rolling wagon to disturb the glaringly bright peace of the Sierra Madre. The older woman continued to glower challengingly at Edge, and the younger one took to mopping at her face with the damp kerchief again.

Edge spat at the dusty trail and took out the makings. He said, "I'm here on my own account, lady, because Delmar Pyle made a sucker out of me and he stole from me. Good chance I wouldn't be this far out on his trail and in such fine shape if it wasn't for you and your buddy. I already told you about how I owe Pyle and you ladies in different ways."

He lit the cigarette with a match struck on the stock of the dead Troy's Winchester.

"We think we know where the swine is headed, Mr. Edge," Dinah blurted.

"And you know he left town with Luis Garcia?"

Just for a second, Harriet Newton was piqued by the exchange. Then she sighed and admitted, "What really worries us is that the two of them could be tied up together in something that'll make suckers out of us—and you." She shot him a nervous glance as she added the tag.

"You have anything hard and fast for that notion to hold on to?" Edge asked evenly.

"The creep has a half share in a gold mine," the redhead answered quickly to beat the younger woman's reply. Then she qualified, "At least, that's what he says. He won it in a poker game in El Paso almost a year ago, he said. He said too he took it as a marker for a thousand dollars. Then the man who owed him against the marker got killed in a saloon brawl.''

''The mine's in Mexico,'' Dinah said. ''Somewhere between Hopeville and San Sarita. So Pyle didn't just happen to come to Wildwood for the gambling. Our town just happened to be on the road to that gold mine of his.''

Edge nodded. ''Somebody back at Wildwood made mention of Hopeville and of gold grubbers from there coming north for the games and the whores.''

''Yeah,'' Harriet confirmed. ''It's between here and San Sarita. A lot closer to the Mexican town than to Wildwood.''

''We been told. Harry and me ain't never been south of the border.''

''We ain't been no place, really,'' the redhead said morosely. ''And we sure don't seem to have learned too much wherever we been.''

Edge pursed his lips and blew out some smoke. ''Sometimes when there's no way of knowing something, you have to try a guess, lady. You have anything stronger than guesswork to tie the banker in with Delmar Pyle?''

''They left town together on Luis Garcia's buckboard,'' Dinah supplied.

''You didn't find that out by reading sign on the trail.''

Harriet replied, ''No. Not everyone in Wildwood thinks we're lower than skunks. One of the whores who came down to the plaza after you went into the cantina spoke to Dinah. She said that after Pyle lost to Troy and the priest, the creep went straight to see Garcia at the bank. And the next thing, they were leaving town on the banker's rig, after Pyle warned people you were a bad loser who'd probably head for Wildwood and make trouble."

"We figured Troy would shoot first and ask questions later," Dinah growled.

"Figured that out for myself after I saw what kind of a feller Troy was and been told what Pyle said about me. What I can't figure is why you ladies should be so worried about Pyle and Garcia heading south on the same rig. And about me finding out about the gold mine."

"I ain't worried none about any of that, Mr. Edge," Dinah assured him earnestly, and shot a glance at Harriet that expressed something akin to guilt. But she was determined to say what was on her mind. "It ain't so easy for Harry, though. She just naturally can't abide men, and she ain't never trusted one of them all her life."

Once more the lean-bodied and thin-faced redhead came near to unleashing an explosion of temper, this time directed at the younger woman who she obviously felt had betrayed a confidence. But then she abruptly drew back from the brink of savage anger and confined herself to an icy brand of scorn as she glowered into the middle distance and added to what her friend had said:

"That's absolutely right. And I ain't making no apology for it. I'm the way I am and there ain't no changing that. And the way I am bothers every man who finds out about me. When they find out they can't screw me one way, they all try to screw me the other way. And Garcia's no different from the rest of the lousy male race. But I needed his lousy bank. The kinda people that live in Wildwood, I wasn't gonna keep no five thousand dollars cash out at the place, with all of them knowing just me and baby lived out there alone. I needed that son of a bitch Pyle. Needed his muscle to do the heavy chores. And now I need someone like you, because you're the kind that can kill and not lose a second of sleep over it. I ain't so much in the brains department, mister. And, like I said already, I ain't been too many places and I ain't learned so very damn much, but in my experience it just ain't safe to trust any man. Use them and get rid of them is how they oughtta be handled, that's my firm opinion. But I'm backed into a lousy corner on this.''

She spat at the wagon's drawpole and deepened the scowl lines in her face as she resumed her cold-eyed study of the ugly images in her memory. ''Pyle was always talking up a storm about getting rich from the gold mine. But he needed a stake so he could look for the claim and work it. It's my belief that with what we'd paid him and what he stole from you, he has enough. And it's my belief also that Garcia has thrown in his lot with Pyle. He's another man that has big ideas about making a killing. That's why he was so eager to help Dinah and me get fixed up in the horse-trading business. I figure Pyle sold him on the gold mine idea, which is how they come to leave town together. The chance of striking it real rich on a claim just has to have more appeal to a man like him than taking care of other people's cash and making a few dollars out of horse dealing.''

She shifted her scornful gaze toward the half-breed. ''And I figure the chance of making a whole pile of money out of a gold mine ain't something a man like you'd turn his back on either, mister. You might throw in your lot with them other two if that creep makes the offer, and if Dinah and me make trouble over it, well, you won't lose no sleep when it comes to killing us.''

"Harry!" the younger woman blurted shrilly, and searched the half-breed's profile with anxious eyes, seeking any hint of rising anger.

Edge dropped the cigarette butt to the barren ground and said, "No sweat, lady."

"She's just upset about everything that's happened, just when it all seemed to be going so well. Harry feels things more than most people do. So she's just bound to be feeling real low now. And you mustn't take no notice of what she says about not trusting you to—"

"I'll start to trust him," the redhead cut in, "when I see him kill that creep Pyle and then ride on about his own business. And that'll be the first time in my life I'll have trusted a man."

Edge nodded, and perhaps there was a glimmer of warmth in his ice-blue eyes as he said through lips drawn back in a quiet smile, "But there are some things a woman just can't ride around—when she's gotta do what a man's gotta do, and can't."

"You'll never know how much it pains me to admit it, mister!" Harriet Newton snarled bitterly.

"Come on, Harry," Dinah McCall urged. "I've never known you to get so low before."

"Just let me alone, baby," the older woman insisted morosely. "Please."

The brunette directed a look of entreaty toward Edge, who offered through the last vestige of a smile, "She just naturally doesn't have what it takes to keep her pecker up."

Chapter Eight

NOBODY SAID anything for a long time. Long enough for the wagon and the horseback rider to cover another slow-moving mile into Sonora.

For a minute or so the older woman nursed resentment at the half-breed's irony, then became detached in a private world of thought. In her introspective mood she appeared to be as content as Edge with the lack of talk. But Dinah was obviously uneasy, as if she mistook the long silence for something the other two never meant it to be. She seemed constantly poised to break it with a question about what was the matter. Or suggest that there was no point in brooding over things now the air had been cleared.

Finally, Dinah brought them together again when she exclaimed, "Oh, my good Lord, what on earth is that?"

Edge had heard the sound in the distance at the same moment as the younger woman and guessed she had probably identified it as easily as he had. He answered, "Somebody crying."

"A woman," Dinah murmured.

Edge had already moved his right hand off the reins to rest it on his thigh, close to where Troy's Winchester jutted from the boot.

"Sharp as they come, the both of you," Harriet growled derisively. "Even I figured that from what I'm hearing. But I ain't hearing nothing that's got me shaking in my frigging boots!"

She abruptly snapped the reins over the backs of the team and yelled at the horses to plunge into a gallop.

"Harry!" Dinah shrieked, and clung to the older woman and the handrail at the side of the seat to keep from being flung off the jolting wagon.

"What I'm hearing is somebody needs help, seems to me!" the redhead yelled, her voice ringing out loud and shrill above the barrage of noise as the wagon raced away in a swirling cloud of dust.

Edge squinted his eyes and compressed his lips against the rising dust. He held back on the urge to curse and drive the gelding into a spurt of speed in the wake of the wagon. Instead, he stroked the neck of his mount with a gentle hand, calming the animal away from the impulse to panic and heeling him forward at the same easy pace as before. Edge watched the wagon disappear around a distant rock face. It was from around this forty-foot-high, sheer wall of weather-scarred granite that the disembodied sound of mournful weeping had floated on the hot, still air.

As Edge rounded the rock face himself, he saw the beginnings of a valley and, down a ways, a shack toward which the wagon was headed, not at such a breakneck speed now. He had his right hand close to the jutting stock of the Winchester while he constantly swept his gaze in every direction.

The small place was sited at the point where the trail came down off the slope and onto the flat bottomland at the start of the valley. The adobe shack, smaller than the one in Dry River Valley and probably with just a single room, looked from a distance to be in a reasonable state of repair, but it lacked any fancy frills. The larger building out back was longer and narrower and seemed to serve, among other things, as a rear boundary marker for the property. The ground between the two buildings and to the sides was neatly planted with lemon trees to the east and vines to the west. Both crops were well tended, with heavy fruit growing amid lush foliage.

Through the heat-hazed air made even less clear by the wagon's dust, Edge saw the twin barrels of a shotgun suddenly thrust out of one glassless window of the shack.

There was nothing in the actions or attitudes of the two women on the wagon seat to suggest they had seen the gun or sensed they were in danger. Dinah McCall had just half turned, peering back up the hill to watch him, while Harriet Newton was slowing the team in front of the shack.

Edge rasped, "Crazy damn women!" He reined the gelding to a standstill with his left hand and smoothly slid the Winchester out of the boot with his right, thumbing back the hammer as part of the same action.

"Harry!" the brunette shrieked, and launched herself to the side to crash into the redhead and take the both of them toppling off the seat of the moving wagon.

Harriet screamed in alarm, both yelled from the forceful impact as they hit the ground.

Meanwhile, the half-breed squeezed off a shot the instant he had the rifle aimed at the window from which the shotgun jutted.

The twin barrels in the adobe house were suddenly angled up at the sky and a hand clutched the window frame. The woman in the shack vented another mournful sound before it was drowned out by a belch of fire and billow of smoke from the shotgun's twin barrels.

The team horses were racing at full gallop by now, plunged into a bolt by the barrage of sounds and lack of restraint. After the thunderous reports, the woman in the shack could still be heard, her wail of despair becoming a roar of rage as the rig hurtled across the front of the shack and down the trail beyond. As the shotgun was jerked back out of sight into the shade, Edge dug in his heels and took up the reins to demand a controlled gallop from the gelding. He pumped the action of the Winchester one-handed as he rode. Flicking his powerful wrist, he arced the barrel through three-quarters of a circle while holding the lever steady.

He was aware of the two women on the ground at the side of the trail some fifty feet away from the shack. Dinah was curled up into a tight ball with her face pressed against her thighs while her arms hugged her ankles. He guessed she was screaming for deliverance while she tried to make herself as small a target as possible. Maybe she was still convinced it was the half-breed who was the threat. Not so Harriet, who had recovered quickly from the shock and pain of being hurled off the wagon and now sat rigidly facing the front of the shack, her slender legs splayed and the big Remington six-shooter thrust out before her at arm's length in a two-handed grip. The redhead was saying

something that was incomprehensible against the hoofbeats and wagon sounds and the yowling of the woman
inside the shack, but Edge knew from the half-profile
view of her thin face that Harriet Newton was mad at
what was happening and wasn't suffering her anger in
silence.

She began to shoot at the window from which the
shotgun had been fired. She did it with firmness and
calm deliberation—by turns squeezing the trigger and
thumbing back the hammer in a measured cadence that
was at cold-blooded odds with the white-hot rage on her
face.

Edge slowed the gelding, poised to take a two-
handed grip on the Winchester again and blast a second
shot into the murky interior of the shack. That was
where the stream of bullets from the Remington was
going, and surely they were not missing their target, for
Harriet Newton was placing her shots with expert
accuracy.

Suddenly the shotgun was sent sailing out over the
ledge. As it hit the ground Edge saw it was still broken
open from a hurried attempt to reload. At the same
time, the wagon slowed a long way out along the trail,
and Edge's chestnut gelding approached the house at an
uneasy walk. The woman inside the shack began to
weep softly, and Dinah McCall raised her face from her
thighs and looked around with blue eyes that were still
crowded with fear. Her pretty mouth was half open, but
only the sound of her fast breathing emerged from it.
Harriet Newton's sparsely fleshed face continued to
express anger that was on the very brink of going out of
control. But she was not so far away from the reality of
the situation that she had failed to realize there were no
more live shells in her revolver.

Edge felt the high tension drain out of him as he reined the gelding to a halt alongside the two women on the ground.

Dinah cried hoarsely, from a throat that sounded as arid as the landscape, "Oh, my good Lord, I thought you was gonna shoot at Harry and me, mister."

"That's crazy, baby," the redhead said flatly, and glanced at Edge to make sure he had the window covered with the Winchester. Then she embraced Dinah as both of them rose unsteadily to their feet. "But the way it turned out, you maybe saved both our lives when you got us off the wagon the way you did."

Edge rode on by them now, the rifle aimed in the general direction of the shack in a one-handed grip. As the acrid taint of black-powder smoke dissipated, he could smell the fresh fragrance of the growing lemons mixed in with the pungent aroma of fermenting wine.

The woman who was weeping abruptly stopped when she saw the half-breed at the window, stooping slightly to look into the cool shade of the simply furnished shack that was not so gloomy at close range. Inside the dim room were three people—the middle-aged, plain-faced woman who looked at Edge as if he were someone from a bad time in her past, and two men. All of them were Mexicans, and just the woman was alive.

"Why did you not kill me, *gringo*?" she asked bitterly from where she sat on the floor, cradling the head of the older dead man in her lap.

"I tried, señora," Edge answered. "But over that kind of distance, I ain't such a hot shot. Then you threw out the gun."

"It will be the great favor if you will kill me now so that I may be with him."

He was aware of the redhead and the brunette coming up on either side of him at the window. Dinah caught her breath and the older woman growled, "Shit, Luis Garcia."

Like the grieving woman's husband, the Wildwood banker had been killed with a blast from the shotgun. Both were caught at close range, with the center of the blast taking the men in the chest. But areas of their faces had been hit too. The man who had grown citrus fruit and grapes had been the more badly disfigured, losing half his jaw so that his gums could be seen with the teeth deeply rooted in them; the eye socket on the same side was only a gory hole in his face. Garcia's face would have looked handsome, except for the pellets that had peppered his complexion.

"The man from the bank," Dinah felt the need to amplify.

"Señor Garcia, he comes with the money to loan my Pablo so that we may build the bigger house," the woman inside blurted, briefly intrigued by the fact that the banker was known to the strangers. But then her voice became as desolate as the expression on her elderly and careworn face as she added, "He brings the *gringo* with him. When the money for the loan is taken from the bag, the *gringo* takes up my Pablo's weapon and shoots them—shoots them like they are the mad dogs that must be . . ."

She broke down into weeping again, her head bent over the shattered face and chest of her husband as she stroked the sparse gray hair at his temples.

"It's him that's the mad dog," Dinah rasped through clenched teeth.

"A son of a bitch is sure what he is," Harriet growled.

"But I never figured him for a killer, Harry," the younger woman murmured, and seemed to find it difficult to wrench her gaze away from the slumped corpse of Luis Garcia.

The new widow began to talk soft and fast to the unresponsive man whose head she nursed so tenderly on her lap. She spoke in her native language, and although her voice was pitched no higher than a conspiratorial whisper, the words carried clearly to the window, where Edge and the two women heard every word.

"Are we just gonna leave the poor woman here like this?" Dinah asked as the half-breed turned from the window and only now eased forward the hammer as he slid the Winchester back in the boot.

"Remember, lady," he said, "it was her, not me, who tried to kill you."

"But she was scared and crazy with grief," Dinah countered. "Harry scared her when she brought the wagon racing down the hill. And the wretched woman has been in the house for Lord knows how long with those dead men. We can't hold it against her that she—"

Edge swung up into his saddle with a finality that drove the woman into uneasy silence. The fast, soft, venomous stream of Mexican continued from within the shack as he gazed down into the upturned faces of the women beside his horse and said flatly, "She wants to kill every living thing in the world to make up for losing her husband. And she wants someone to kill her. I want to kill only Delmar Pyle. This is just a place he's been and gone from."

"She's out of her mind right now. Surely we can help her for a few minutes with getting—"

Edge shrugged as he took up the reins, and the distraught younger woman realized he would never agree to what she wanted. She wrenched her head around to direct an entreating gaze at the redhead, but Harriet Newton showed no more sympathy than the half-breed as she began to turn the cylinder and eject the spent cartridges from the chambers of the revolver. She said dully, "I wanted to help her, baby, but we don't have the time to waste consoling her. Take this gun if you want to put her out of her misery. Long as you're sure you can live with yourself after."

Edge tugged gently on the reins and touched his heels to turn the gelding and head him along the trail toward the stalled wagon some half mile distant. He did not ride so fast that the redhead had to hurry to keep up, but at first the younger woman needed to run a few paces in order to reach her partner and fall in beside her. Then, during a silence that lasted for several seconds, she cast mournful glances back over her shoulder toward the shack, where the widow had either stopped making empty vows to the dead man or had lowered her voice.

"Look at it this way, baby," Harriet offered at length as Edge took the makings from a shirt pocket. "She's feeling at her lowest right now, hating the whole rotten world. But when time's healed her some, I figure she'll appreciate that we took care of the son of a bitch that murdered her husband."

Dinah shook her head, but she wasn't denying the truth of what the other woman had said. "Not *us*, Harry," she corrected, and interlocked her arm with that of the redhead as she glowered at the back of the easy-riding half-breed. "I know you could've killed that woman. I heard you and saw you. But you ain't the type to—"

"It's what I want to do and what I hired on to do, lady," Edge said without turning around as he hung the cigarette at the side of his mouth.

"I could've sure enough," Harriet said, detached but grim-faced as she recalled the frenetic moments when she emptied her pistol in a blind rage at an unseen target.

The younger woman, abruptly and uncharacteristically the stronger partner, unlinked her arm and took a firmer and more reassuring grip around the waist of the redhead, insisting, "Forget it, Harry. I guess we can all do awful things in that kind of temper. But that ain't nearly the same as what that son of a bitch Pyle done in cold blood back there."

Harriet sighed and attempted to put self-doubt out of her mind. "That's something I can't take a grip on," she muttered. "That creep's a liar and a cheat and a pervert and a whole lot of other lousy things, but I had him figured as a coward to boot. Just can't see him picking up a shotgun and—"

"You never know what kind of animal instincts you'll unleash in a man if you bury him up to his collar, lady," Edge cut in as he struck a match on the rifle stock and lit the cigarette. "Could be a mad dog or an ice-cold bastard."

He shook out the flame and arced the dead match to the ground as he reined the gelding in beside the wagon where the sweat-lathered horses were still breathing heavily in their traces.

"Figure there ain't no doubt about what kind you are, mister," Dinah McCall snapped as the redhead went to the bolt-wearied horses and took off her forage cap to wipe the foam from their coats. "You wanna tell us what made you the way—"

"Let it be, baby," Harriet advised.

"No sweat," Edge drawled, and drew back his lips in a cold smile. "Guess you could say I've been in the doghouse ever since people found out my bite's worse than my bark."

Chapter Nine

THROUGHOUT THE remainder of the morning and into the middle of the afternoon, the trail through the Sierra Madre continued to show clearly that another wagon and two-horse team had headed south earlier in the day. The tracks made by the shod hooves and the iron-rimmed wheels were clearly imprinted in the dust.

Once, Edge broke the long silence to say in an unconcerned manner, "The prospectors have to make a long trip to get to Wildwood."

"San Sarita's even farther away than Hopeville," Harriet Newton answered dully. "So the Federales have the worst of it."

Later, when the sun was at the top of its arc across the Mexican sky, blazing its broiling heat down on the rugged mountain country, Dinah McCall said, "I could sure do with a rest from riding this hard seat."

"Horses are in need of a breather too," Edge replied. "Looking for a spot to halt right now."

At the stopping place he chose in the warm shade of a crazily leaning slab of rock, he and the women chewed on some jerked beef and washed it down with canteen water that tasted like it was at blood heat. Toward the end of the spartan meal, Harriet said with a shake of her head, "To my mind, there can't be much that's worse than loneliness."

"Guess that's sure enough why the prospectors and the Federales go all the way to Wildwood and back when they got the money for it," the younger woman answered.

"Was thinking about the widow back up the trail, baby. Looked like her and her husband put a lot of time and hard work into the place. Were making a go of it. But if I was in her place—if it was you that got killed . . ." She shook her head again. "Well, something worse than just being lonely is being alone in a place you used to share, I guess. Share with . . ."

Edge refixed the stopper into the neck of the canteen and got up off his haunches.

"What's eating you, mister?" the younger woman asked irritably, still in the unusual position of being the stronger of the two women.

"An urge to kill Delmar Pyle," he told her as he began to resaddle his briefly rested horse. "And it'll keep on gnawing away at me until the maggots are eating him."

Perhaps an hour later, as the wagon and its escorting rider entered the narrow mouth of a canyon, the redhead asked, "You ever shared something with someone and had it end suddenly, Edge?"

"Yeah, lady," the half-breed replied. And there was a degree of hardness in his tone that warned the women that Harriet had touched one of the man's rawest nerves.

But while they waited anxiously for an explosion of anger from him, it seemed ever more likely that he wasn't going to expand on his reply. Just as they thought he had nothing more to say, he went on in a more even tone, "I was sharing a long run of peace and quiet with the world, and then I found the feller you buried on your place."

The women knew that his caustic irony was a convenient cover for something he had been on the verge of revealing about himself. Each guessed that the secret he continued to keep involved a woman, even a wife. But when he was through with the glib and brief explanation, he shot them each a cold, glittering gaze that warned he had said all he was going to on the subject.

"All right, mister, I'll mind my own business," Harriet promised, with no hint of rancor.

"And if you had minded yours," Dinah said to Edge, "and not interfered with the hard time we gave that swine, none of this would've happened!"

"Meant to ask you about that," Edge replied, still even toned, refusing to be baited by the younger, prettier woman and aware that Harriet Newton had been trying to convey something like gratitude to him. "Was there a particular reason you did that to him?"

"He said that the worst thing that could happen to him was to be buried alive," Dinah replied eagerly, and then put a degree of pique back in her tone as she realized she was in danger of losing the attention of the impassive man riding at the side of the wagon. "Not right there and then, after he tried to do that to me. It was when we were talking over supper one night. As we were talking back and forth, we got around to what we hated the most. What we figured was the worst could happen to us."

Part of Edge's attention was attracted by the faint smell of meat burning that was being carried on the wind. That meant people. But there was something odd about the aroma, and there was no sign of smoke in the distance.

"Pyle started the conversation on that subject, of course," Harriet Newton said, taking up the tale in a detached way. "Trying to get it out of baby and me that for a man to put his hands on us that way was what we wanted. The suggestion was enough to make us sick to our stomachs. After that, he told us being buried alive was the thought that made him break out into a cold sweat. We never told him about our secret fears, did we, baby? But then he'd already made up his mind. And I guess the idea of having a woman that didn't want to be taken by any man . . ."

She let the suggestion hang incomplete and shrugged her slim shoulders.

"Don't guess there's a thing you'd admit to be that afraid of, mister?" Dinah challenged.

"Except death," Harriet put in absently as she came out of her reverie.

"Death doesn't scare me that much," Edge corrected, and ran a finger along his brow to wipe away the beads of sweat.

"So how come you're so jittery about having guns aimed at you?" Harriet asked, and there was genuine interest in her voice and eyes, while the younger woman's sneer showed her opinion of what she considered to be nothing more than Edge's tough talk.

"There's a special reason, lady," the half-breed answered with no loss of composure, though he was recalling a long-dead brother and a wife who was dead a long time too. "But I've lived for so long by being scared of the process of dying."

"For Pete's sake!" Dinah complained impatiently. "Death and dying and that kinda stuff scares all of us. And I guess you could say that being buried alive is a way of dying that bothered that swine."

Edge spoke sternly: "Ain't never been in a situation where I was so hungry I had to eat human meat, but I figure right now that's what would—"

Wisps of dark smoke now smudged the slick grayness of the distant heat shimmer. As Edge wrinkled his nostrils after his remark on cannibalism, both women stared ahead along the trail and caught the smell of cooking meat at the same time as they saw the smoke that was carrying the fragrance.

"Smells like roast pork to me," the younger woman said, but it was patently just bravado that kept her from showing the same degree of horror as was displayed on the thinner and less pretty face of the redhead.

"Mr. Edge?" Harriet said.

"Been a long time since I smelled it, lady. Not just the one time. In the war. Indian troubles. Other troubles. It always smells like roast pork."

"Oh, my God!" the redhead gasped, and threw a hand up to her mouth, fighting back the vomit rising in her throat.

The younger woman came even closer to throwing up as the image conjured up by the half-breed suddenly came to life in her mind. Both of them found it necessary to screw their eyes tightly shut as they compressed their lips, and their throats pumped frantically in a fight for air and a struggle against something more palpable.

Then Edge saw the funeral pyre burning fiercely a short way off the side of the trail as it ran out of the southern end of the canyon. But he said nothing to the women as the wagon team continued to clop along the arrow-straight trail, unconcerned by the looseness of the reins in the grip of Harriet Newton. The horses were perhaps too weary from the long trek to react with more than the flare of nostrils to the sweet smell of burning. Certainly his own mount was not unduly disturbed by the fire some five hundred feet off the trail in front of a cavernlike hole in the base of the canyon wall.

The elongated fire, some eight by two feet, was fueled by large sections of timber which burned with a constant, high-reaching flame. It seemed to Edge that the wood had been impregnated with a combustible preservative. The tongues of flame—yellow, blue, green, and red—leapt within the dense black smoke that swirled upward for just a few feet before being captured and flung to the sides by capricious air currents. The smoke wasn't so thick at its source that it totally obscured the corpse that was being cremated by the blaze, a corpse that was already a charred effigy of a human form as it sagged between a supporting frame at each end of the fire. The figure was black from lashed ankles to bound wrists, except for lengths of white or gray bone that showed where the scorched flesh had fallen away from the skeleton. There was no crimson tissue to be seen; the heat had vaporized the blood, and the smoke had sooted the dried-out flesh.

It was apparent, even from a distance, that the cross-angled struts were of metal and the bonds that trapped the corpse between them were of tough wire. It was a construction intended to withstand the fierceness of the flames.

"Oh, my good Lord," Dinah McCall rasped from a throat that was parched dry by horror.

"If the meat's for supper, it's already overdone," Edge said evenly, and tugged on the reins to veer his mount off the trail, heading him toward the pyre.

"You're disgusting!" the younger woman accused, then she swung anxiously around on the seat as the redhead uttered a strangled moan when she saw and recognized what was strung up over the fire. "Pay him no mind, Harry," Dinah hurried on, failing to express on her pretty face the degree of reassuring composure she managed to falsify in her tone. In a moment she took the team reins that had been surrendered by Harriet, who needed both hands to squeeze at her throat and trap the rising vomit. "He's acting up tough again is all. Trying to make you feel——"

"Drive us over there, baby," the older woman interrupted, her gaze fixed on the smoky area ahead of the lone rider. There was a mechanical quality about her voice that perfectly matched the rigidity of her attitude on the seat, and Dinah had only to glance at her to know it would be futile to argue.

Dinah steered the wagon off the trail and drove along a line that converged with Edge's path. The cloyingly sweet smell got stronger, the smoke thickened and hung lower and longer before the air currents claimed it, and the heat grew more intense. The women took their example from the half-breed and raised the kerchiefs from around their necks to mask their mouths and nostrils.

A man, wraithlike on the far side of the smoke and heat shimmer of the flames, vented a gust of belly laughter as he emerged from the opening in the canyon wall. Edge, who had been riding with just one hand on the reins, brought his mount to an instant standstill and took a firmer grip on the booted rifle some forty feet from the fire. Dinah McCall kept the wagon rolling for a few more moments before the older woman reclaimed control of the team and brought the rig to a halt. During the nerve-racking seconds of silence, the man took three staggering steps and came to a swaying stop with his legs splayed and his arms hanging limply down at his sides. A moment before he spoke, his head lolled so that his chin hit his chest and he seemed in danger of toppling forward toward the fire.

"If you guys are the holdup men, you sure as hell . . ." His voice was slurred and confirmed what had seemed likely from his wavering gait and unsteady stance: he was drunk and perhaps more than a little crazy too. Now, after he had belched, he was able to finish: "You sure as hell look like them, but you're too friggin' late. The bastard took me and Curtis for every last cent we had. Or if it's gold you come for, are you outa luck! But at least you didn't have to break your balls diggin' to find how bad you lucked out! Like me and Curtis!"

His voice got louder as his tone became more bitter. His stance was solid and he was able to hold up his head by the time he finished speaking, but he was less distinctly seen through the smoke which now rose several feet toward the Mexican sky before it was gently disturbed by the lazily moving air currents. By the same token, the man on the far side of the fire was unable to see the newcomers as clearly as before.

But the skinny old man with a bald head and a livid scar on his right cheek could have an instinct for danger, so Edge retained his grip on the frame of the Winchester but made no move to slide it out of the boot. The ice-blue slits of his eyes above the kerchief mask glittered in fixed concentration upon the shadowy form beyond the fire, seeking a first move of the man's right hand, the one in which a revolver was gripped. The half-breed had seen at the outset that the man's left fist was tight around the neck of an almost full bottle of clear liquid.

"We don't want nothing—" Dinah began.

"The masks are to keep out some of the stink of what you're doing to Curtis, feller," Edge cut in, and his monotone sounded colder than it was in contrast with the woman's shrill nervousness.

He heard the redhead rasp a silencing curse at the brunette just before the man across the pyre vented another harsh laugh. It was much shorter this time and so lacking in mirth that Dinah's moan of disgust could have been an echo of it.

"If you reckon Curtis Webster smells bad now, folks, you oughtta have shared these here diggin's with him when he was alive and kickin'." Then he shook his head and spat at the fire, which was built of tunnel support beams. "Still, I guess I ain't the one to cast no first stones. Anyone workin' out in this lousy country just can't help stinkin', and ain't nothin' special about me."

"Feller named Delmar Pyle kill your partner?" Edge asked.

"*Feller* nothin'!" the man snarled. "You're talkin' stinks, mister! That lyin', cheatin' . . . Why, that ain't nothin' but a skunk that stood up on its hind legs and learned how to walk! Why, I ain't never—"

"Much obliged," the half-breed cut in, and made to pull on the reins and head his uneasy gelding away from the smoke and the cloyingly sweet fragrance.

"Hey, wait on there, you folks! Stay awhile and give me a hand to send off old Curtis the way he wanted. Have a few slugs of tequila. Talk some. Sing some if you've a mind. It's what old Curtis always said he wanted to happen when he was dead and gone. And made me promise somethin' else way back. That if we was out in this kinda country when his number come up, then I was to cremate him. Way I'm doin' right now.''

"Way he was afraid of being buried alive, figure the feller that killed him could have the same burning ambition," Edge said.

"What's that?" the old-timer wanted to know, head cocked to one side.

"Forget it, mister!" Dinah McCall snarled through the smoke. "He likes to be the life and soul of the party with them kinda cracks that nobody else reckons are so damn—"

"Ain't no party!" Curtis Webster's bereft partner suddenly bellowed. "It's a wake, that's what it is! Just on account of I'm takin' a slug or two in memory of old Curtis, ain't no reason for you men to say I'm havin' a party!"

From the manner in which the corpse had been fixed over the elongated fire, it was the rear end of Curtis Webster that hung the lowest in the flames and burned the fastest. Thus it was in this area that his skeleton first began to snap apart as the tissue in the joints submitted to the searing heat and both hip joints separated within a second of each other, each with a distinctive cracking sound. Then, a moment later, the few shreds of flesh that still kept the former man in one piece at the waist were unable to support even his much diminished weight and his frame separated into two pieces, each contributing to the billowing eruption of smoke and sparks as it flopped into the fire.

As the old-timer raised the bottle of tequila to take

another drink, Harriet Newton glimpsed the movement through the smoke and misinterpreted it.

"Baby!" she shrieked, and snatched the Remington from her holster as she powered to her feet on the wagon and shot into the thick veil of spark-speckled smoke.

Unconcerned that the man's left hand had moved, Edge had again been about to head his horse away from the stinking fire, but the sound of fear-filled urgency in Harriet Newton's voice stayed his hand on the reins and sent his other hand streaking toward the booted rifle. The Winchester was almost clear when he heard the crack of the bullet as it left the revolver muzzle.

He rasped, "Oh shit, lady."

His fast double take at the old-timer revealed that the handgun in the man's right hand was still hanging low down at his side while his left was still held high as it brought the bottle neck within an inch of his lips. Just before the smoke obscured the scene again, the man's teeth snapped together to display a snarl of rage in the wake of the gunshot.

Edge started to bring his head around as the first words of a shouted warning formed in his throat. But it was too late. Another shot cracked out, and the old-timer collected a long overdue stroke of good furtune as the bullet he exploded through the curtain of smoke drilled a hole in the side of Dinah McCall's face between her left ear and eye. It passed just inches above Harriet Newton's shoulder as the older woman flung herself across the front of Dinah in a desperate and doomed effort to act as a human shield.

The half-breed glimpsed what he knew could only be a fatal wound, seeing it only on the periphery of his vision at the same time he saw the thin face of the redhead express the sure and certain knowledge that her friend was going to die.

Then, the rifle clear of the boot and thudded against his shoulder, Edge began to blast shot after shot through the smoke. In his attitude was something of the cool deliberation with which Harriet Newton had emptied her handgun through a window into a room she could not see. But Edge spoke no word, nor was there a flicker of expression on his thickly bristled, sweat-beaded face. It was a basic, uncomplicated kill-or-be-killed situation, which existed for the time it took Edge to blast four bullets from the Winchester before the smoke curtain briefly thinned and he was able to see the old-timer again. The man seemed older and thinner and sadder now that he was sprawled out on his back with a dark stain blossoming over the fabric of his long johns at the center of his chest. His right hand was palm up and splayed, the gun it had held nowhere in sight. His left was still in a tight grip around the neck of the tequila bottle, which was spilling some of its contents. Despite the distorting effect of the smoke and shimmering heat, which made it seem as if the man was trembling, Edge recognized the old man was in the grip of death. As far as the half-breed could tell, he had been hit in the chest by just one bullet. Edge could not see, at this distance, if the killing shot was one of his or the single bullet Harriet Newton had fired. It was certain that the hapless old-timer had himself only managed to get off the one fatal bullet before his own end came.

"My baby's dead," the lean redhead said dully.

Edge looked at the wagon and saw that the positions of the two women had been reversed while his attention was diverted. Now the older one was sitting upright, and Dinah McCall was slumped across her lap. Blood from the small hole in the brunette's temple seeped slowly out and stained both the bare forearms on which her head was cradled.

"Same as the feller who killed her," the half-breed countered evenly, making a conscious effort to stay icily calm. "Now all we have to do is get the one that planned for her to have a fate worse than death."

In the long seconds after the violent end of the woman who had been more than a friend to her, Harriet Newton was more emotionally controlled than she had ever been in her life. There had been no sorrow when she spoke of Dinah's dying and now not a trace of either anger or bitterness as she told the half-breed, "What Pyle tried to do to her wasn't funny, mister."

She was coolly in control as she made the monotone reprimand. However, she had lost that part of his attention that had not been devoted to taking shells from a saddlebag to load into the rifle's depleted magazine. The focus of his narrowed eyes had lenghtened to look far beyond the wagon, and she slowly turned her head, taking great care not to disturb Dinah McCall's body. She peered back into the canyon and saw that Edge was watching another rig as it emerged from the distant heat haze. As yet it was too far off to be seen as more than a slow-moving blur against the glare of the sun-filled canyon.

As she returned her gaze to the half-breed, she gently took one of her arms from beneath the head of the dead woman to tug the kerchief mask off her lower face. He saw, as he slid the reloaded rifle into the boot and swung out of the saddle, that there was just the faintest of tics working at the corner of her mouth.

"You don't have to act so tough, Harry," he told her. "Even real men get to cry sometimes."

"Right now I'm sorry about just one thing, mister," she answered. "You wanna know what that is?"

"Figure I'm going to be told."

He went around to the other side of the funeral pyre, and she could see him as he went down on his haunches close to the sprawled corpse of the old-timer. Heat shimmer and smoke continued to have a distorting effect on everything beyond the fire, so it was not until he returned that she was able to see he had appropriated the dead man's revolver and the bottle of tequila that was now less than half full. The pistol was in Edge's tied-down holster, and he was wiping the neck of the bottle with the palm of his hand as he emerged from behind the fire.

"What I'm real sorry about," she went on more heatedly as he pulled the kerchief off his face, "is that the old creep who laughed so easy is dead. Figure he might've found your lousy cracks funny, mister. Still, maybe whoever's coming down the trail will be in a better mood to . . ." The tic began to get more pronounced as she spoke her meandering comments, and grief struggled with anger as her self-control started to crack. First spasming affected one entire side of her face and then sobs of anguish forced her words to falter. Edge took a slow drink from the bottle as he waited to see if the redhead could get a grip on her composure again. She did, sufficiently to tell him with scowling vehemence, "But I'll have to be sure to tell them to be careful they don't die laughing, mister! Life and soul of the party, my . . ."

Everything that had been pent up inside her suddenly poured out as she embraced the limp form of the dead woman and her tears flowed with greater force than had the life blood of the younger woman. As he watched, Edge lowered the bottle from his lips and slowly shook his head with an expression almost of remorse.

Chapter Ten

IT WAS the emaciated priest from Wildwood who drove the creaking, clattering, badly cared for buggy off the trail and across to where the redhead wept herself dry of tears and the half-breed took occasional sips of tequila. Beside him in the shade of the roof was the plain-faced, middle-aged, cried-out widow of the fruit farmer and wine maker named Pablo.

The woman, who was hatless and had changed out of the bloodstained dress into another of the same gray color and shapelessness, took in all aspects of the scene as the four-wheeled rig hauled by a single elderly-looking gray gelding rolled to a halt alongside the flatbed. Her dark eyes moved between their red and puffed rims and her nostrils briefly flared as they detected the now diminished fragrance of Webster's burned corpse. But she was still too concerned with the anguish of her own grief to have emotion to spare for the suffering of others, and having made her undemonstrative survey of the carnage spread before her, she withdrew into a state of detachment that seemed close to a catatonic trance.

Father Felipe Chevez was slightly more expressive as he made the sign of the cross at his chest after sweeping a shocked gaze over the area of carnage beneath the drifting smoke. Showing pity in the wake of horror, he needed to swallow several times before he was able to ask, "Pyle again, señor? This is more of his evil?"

"Not all of it, feller," Edge replied evenly. He ran the back of a hand along his lips as he eyed the bottle ruefully, then hurled it hard enough into the fire to smash the glass.

"He killed the man called Curtis Webster," Harriet Newton amplified as she slowly eased out from under the weight of the corpse of Dinah McCall. Then she tenderly allowed the body to slump sideways across the seat, taking care that it did not roll off onto the footboard as the wagon moved on its springs while she climbed down. "Pyle shot Webster in an argument over a card game, I think. Webster'd told his partner he wanted to be cremated if he died out here in Sonora. His partner was doing that when we showed up. His partner was drunk. There was a misunderstanding. My mistake. I couldn't see properly through the smoke. I shot first. I thought he was bringing up his gun to shoot at us. But he was just taking a drink, that's all."

While she offered the explanation of what had happened, she seemed once again to be devoid of emotion, but she spoke distinctly against the crackling of the fire that now had just wood and bone to consume. As she climbed up onto the rear of the wagon and started to free the burlap sheet, her movements were mechanically deliberate so that it was patently obvious she herself knew she was on a mental tightrope.

"He shot back. I can't blame him for that. He killed Dinah. And then Edge killed him. Edge can't be blamed. Nor me, is how I see it. Hadn't been for Delmar Pyle, none of this would've happened. None of—"

She had intended to gesture toward the mournfully stoic Mexican woman who remained on the seat of the buggy as the priest climbed down, but found her attention captured by the half-breed as he swung up astride his saddle.

"This place is like three others I've got to since this thing began, lady," Edge said into the questioning pause she left. "Just another stop he made before he moved on."

"But I can't leave baby here!" the redhead countered, her tone rising. She struggled to pitch it lower as she went on, coldly defiant now, "And I sure as hell wouldn't think of traveling with her spread out over the wagon seat the way she is."

Chevez, his head bowed and slowly shaking from side to side, had gone to the far side of the fire. His hands were clasped tightly together at the base of his belly in a way that suggested silent prayer. Or maybe he was standing that way to keep his hands and body from trembling.

"Padre?" Edge called as he dug into a shirt pocket for the makings.

The hatless, cassocked priest completed his circuit of the fire and the sprawled corpse beyond it. The profound look in his sunken eyes as he emerged from the smoke contained no query.

"It is Calvin Terry, *eficazmente*," he announced. "He and Señor Webster have been *compañeros* for a long, long time. Both were *anciano*—old, but not yet ready for *muerte*."

In fast, toneless Mexican, the woman in his buggy told the priest that her husband hadn't been ready to die either. Chevez made to disengage his hands from each other, but was quick to clasp them tight again. He bobbed his head.

"*Sí, sí.* Pablo Banales had much to live for. Likewise Luis Garcia." He gave a shrug of his skinny shoulders. "None of the creatures of *Dios* should be struck down so tragically. And for mere *dinero.*"

"I was going to ask you what you did about the two men Pyle shot back at the farm, feller," Edge said as he completed rolling the cigarette. He elected to speak American for the sake of the redhead, rather than the native language of his father which he had picked up during his youth on the Iowa farmstead.

"What I did, señor?" Chevez was puzzled.

"About their corpses," Edge added as he struck a match on the butt of his newly acquired Navy Colt.

"Ah, *sí.*" The priest bobbed his head again. "Señora Banales had already done as much as she was able before I reached the farm, señor. I could do no more than pray for the souls of *los difuntos* and bring Señora Banales to San Sarita to make the arrangements with the funeral director. The matter of where Luis Garcia is to be buried . . ." He parted his hands now and exhibited the palms in a gesture of confusion. "We shall see."

During the exchange between the two men, Harriet Newton had continued with her self-imposed chores on the back of the wagon. She had taken blankets from her own and the other woman's bedrolls and spread them on the area of the wagon bed behind the heap of freight. Now, with a fund of strength called upon out of necessity, she eased the corpse over the back rest of the seat and onto the blankets, doing this with the same kind of tender care she would have shown had Dinah McCall been alive but helpless.

"I ain't gonna have baby buried in a foreign country," she proclaimed as she began to wrap the body in the blankets. "Not in some godforsaken nowhere place like this. Or even in some regular graveyard in a regular town. Gonna take her back to our place in Dry River Valley and—"

She broke off what she was saying to stare at Edge with a mixture of confused forlornness and waning defiance. This as he brought his mount around in a slow about-face wheel.

"One thing you can be sure of: if I never get back to your part of the country, lady," he told her, and touched a forefinger lightly to the brim of his hat, "I won't give up on this until either me or Pyle is dead."

"But you can't leave me here!" she complained. "We got a deal!" I have to be there and see—"

"There's one way I'll wait for you in San Sarita," he cut in on her, "Do what the widow is doing. Leave Dinah here with Calvin Terry until—"

"No!" Defiance was paramount again. "I told you I won't do that! I'm not going to leave baby!" She experienced revulsion as she swept a glance back along the canyon, then peered out over the mesa of the high plain to the south. Finally she glowered up at the hazy sky as she challenged, "I ain't going to leave her out here for the coyotes and the buzzards to . . ."

She quaked again, then gave a choked sob that seemed to warn of more to come if she did any more of this kind of talking.

"Señorita, we can be in town in less than an hour," Chevez said as Harriet Newton completed the shrouding of the body. The undertaker can be here in another

127

hour. If the remains of your friend are left in the mine where I intend to place those of Señor Terry, no harm can be—''

''I won't have her buried in Mexico! I already said—''

''*Sí, señorita*,'' the priest cut in, his tone patient but with a weary frown on his gaunt face. ''Whatever you wish, it can be so arranged. But you and Señor Edge have business elsewhere, you say. If this takes much time to complete, the remains will . . .'' He left the warning incomplete and shrugged his narrow shoulders.

The widow in the buggy complained in even-toned Mexican that they had wasted enough time with the *gringos* and should be moving on about their own business with the San Sarita undertaker. The priest nodded and supplemented this with a reassuring hand gesture, then gave inquiring looks to the impassive Edge, who remained on the brink of riding away, and the grieving redhead, who was now securing the blankets with ropes. Then he returned to the far side of the fire where he started to drag the body of Calvin Terry toward the mine entrance.

''They're going to leave pretty soon, lady,'' the half-breed said. ''I'll be gone before they do.''

Scorn glittered through the sorrow in her cool green eyes as she peered at his compassionless face and the cigarette angled from the side of his mouth. She accused, ''You just don't care, do you?''

''Not when I don't have to, lady,'' he told her. ''And right now the only thing I care about is seeing Delmar Pyle gets what's coming to him. I'll wait in San Sarita until the priest and his passenger reach there. Whether you're with them or not, I'll—''

''Wait!'' she snarled as he heeled the gelding forward.

He looked toward her but made no attempt to rein in

his mount. He scowled faintly when he saw the woman come upright on the wagon, her right hand reaching for her hip holster. Her scowl expressed a more explosive brand of anger as her curled fingers failed to find the expected Remington. Then the realization hit her that she had discarded the revolver when she saw Dinah McCall was dead.

"No day's all bad," Edge said coldly. "Least you get to stay alive."

"What's so damn good about that?" she demanded, then checked her anger and sounded close to plaintive as she called after him, "I'm gonna leave baby here, mister! It'll just take a couple of minutes or so! Then we can go on together!"

Edge continued to ride inexorably away from the scene of his latest encounter with violence and did not look back at one woman standing in the blazing sun on the rear of the wagon, a blanket-wrapped corpse at her feet, and another sitting in the shade of the buggy roof, peering at the unrecognizable remains of the man that had been burned on the pyre. The priest emerged from the hole in the cliff face beyond the fire, rubbing his palms down the sides of his cassock as if to wipe them clean of some palpable trace of death picked up from handling the body that was now stowed in the mine.

"Please, mister!" Harriet Newton implored in a quaking voice. "For God's sake, wait for me!"

"I fear, señorita, that such a man has not the faith." Father Felipe Chevez spoke without raising his voice, but his doleful tones were discernable to the slow-riding half-breed against the clop of the gelding's hooves and the crackling of the fire. "I fear he has not the faith in God. And so to call upon the Almighty in such a—"

Harriet Newton swore, and the widow in the buggy

muttered impatiently at the priest. One or both women caused Chevez to abandon what he was saying, after which Edge showed a respect of sorts by taking the cigarette out of his mouth as he looked skyward and murmured, ''We know different, huh? I treat people the way they treat me. And since I'm still alive and kicking, I guess You still have some faith in me.''

Chapter Eleven

EDGE MADE an initial survey of San Sarita with a mood of ill humor dragging down the corners of his thin-lipped mouth. If anyone had been close enough to see his slitted eyes glinting like ice, they would surely have presumed the dirty, unshaven, disheveled rider was giving his first reaction to the town.

This misinterpretation would have been understandable, for the town was an unbeautiful place, and seen closer at hand, it became increasingly ugly.

The first town on the trail into Mexico was built on the southern rim of a band of high plain, a piece of terrain that was less barren and more rugged than the desert, featuring as it did sagebrush and cactus and even the occasional stand of stunted trees among mesas and knolls and rock outcrops of all shapes and sizes. According to a sun-bleached timber signpost a mile or so back, it was not the first community south of the border. That had been Hopeville, off the trail to the west.

After leaving the pyre at the mine entrance, Edge had demanded a canter from his mount. But he had not asked for such speed for long in the broiling heat of afternoon. He had more respect for the animal that had served him so well for so long. He had felt a compelling need, though, to be apart from all human contact for a while in the hope that during the hour or so the priest said it would take to reach San Sarita he would achieve some peace of mind.

San Sarita had a more formal plaza than Wildwood—a square with a cluster of barely alive trees at the center. The trail Edge was on became a street that entered the square on the north side; two other streets came in from the east and west. Adobe buildings, all one story but of various shapes and sizes, were spread along both sides of the three streets for about a quarter mile. At the end of the street to the east was a church and cemetery and then the terrain became ruggedly steep to both the east and south. To the west the trail opened up again, curving to the south and rising steeply in a series of sharp curves. Flanking the trail up the mountain were fields of cotton, tobacco, and corn and some scrub pasture on which a few small herds of cattle grazed. Neither the crops nor the livestock looked very healthy, and the peons working in the fields seemed, from a distance, to move with a degree of lethargy that suggested something more than the weariness that could be expected toward the end of a day's labor under the searingly hot sun. Certainly the old men, the women of all ages, and the children who eyed Edge with hostility from in and around the dilapidated houses as he rode into town looked sick from emaciation and exhaustion, and maybe disease.

He did not return their scrutiny with anything like the

intensity they showed toward him, for he didn't sense any threat from these people, only the futile anger of poverty.

Down on the plaza was a group of six men, more prosperous looking than any of the San Sarita citizens in and around the houses. They sat on some benches in the sparse shade of the gnarled, twisted cottonwoods at the center of the plaza. Sombreros shaded them more effectively than the spartan foliage of the trees, but not so darkly that Edge was unable to see that the men were all between fifty and sixty, reasonably well-groomed, and almost finely clothed in a mixture of Mexican- and American-style shirts, pants, boots, vests, and belts. A pall of smoke from their cigars hung above them, and they eyed Edge through the aromatic haze without hostility. Instead, each man seemed to be appraising him.

After a glance around the buildings that lined the plaza, the half-breed knew what lay behind the open curiosity: each of the town's more affluent citizens was wondering if there were some Yankee dollars to be made out of the newcomer to their community.

As he rode to the center of the plaza, the half-breed was able to see along each of the side streets and confirm his first impressions. The street that led to the church was where such men as the local merchants lived, and the one that curved away to the south from the western side was flanked by houses of the poor.

"*Buenas tardes, señor,*" one of the men who had been engaged in a game of two-handed poker said as Edge reined his horse to a standstill.

The half-breed nodded, and the other player and the four watchers of the game nodded and displayed tentative smiles.

"Welcome to San Sarita," one of the observers said in American. "If there is any way we can be of service, señor? You see we own the businesses that you see. . . ."

He gestured with a hand to encompass the commercial premises on three sides of the plaza. But he left his sales spiel on behalf of the town's merchants unfinished when he saw that the stranger's scowling attention was directed toward the Federale post that was on the south side of the plaza.

From where he sat his horse beside the cottonwoods, Edge could see just the roofs of two buildings and the part of the impressive facade of the post that was not obscured by a fifteen-foot-high wall across the front and sides. The green, white, and red flag of Mexico hung limply from a mast midway between the post gateway and the portico of the main two-story building, and there was some faded lettering along the lintel above the gates that, when it was newly painted, had proclaimed the property the headquarters of the Mexican Federales in this region of the state of Sonora. It was not only the legend above the gateway that had been allowed to deteriorate, though. The front wall was bulging in some places and crumbling in others. And it had been a long time since anyone had taken the trouble to obliterate the antigovernment slogans daubed on it.

"Appears my most pressing business is with the Federale comandante," Edge replied absently as he heeled his horse forward.

There were some muttered obscenities and a few loud expectorations from the group of businessmen, obviously all expressions of ill feeling at the man in charge of the Federale post. Then, as a demand was made for the card game to be restarted, the spokesman of the bunch advised, "Comandante Gomez is out of town, señor."

"When the organ grinder ain't around, a feller has to make do with the monkey," Edge growled as he rode out of the late afternoon shade and approached the gates of the post.

The gates were more rust-colored than their original black, and apparently the lock no longer worked, for a length of chain held them shut. Close to the gates, the half-breed was able to get a better view of what had once been a fine house and adjacent outbuildings before they had been adapted for use as a Federale post. Set in the center of a walled garden, the Spanish colonial-style mansion had perhaps thirty rooms. Tramping feet in Mexican-government-issue boots had long since reduced all but one tiny section of the garden to hard-packed dirt on which nothing grew—the exception being a small circular area at the base of the flagpole in which a few straggling weeds clung tenaciously to life.

The house and the stable block to one side had suffered from the same lack of care as the wall and gates, but because of the surrounding defenses, the slogan painters had not been able to deface the crumbling stucco and weathered adobe. The other two-story building that he had seen from the center of the plaza was a barracks block that ran from the front to the rear at one side of the post. A few other buildings, as inelegantly designed and badly constructed as the barracks, had been erected since the private property was given over to military use.

"What do you want, *gringo*?"

The Federale corporal swung into view from the wall to the half-breed's left as he snapped the query. It came as no surprise to Edge, for he had seen tobacco smoke

135

wafting across the gateway. The corporal, who was the only man in sight beyond the entrance, was too tall and skinny for his drab gray uniform, which was creased and stained and had two badly sewn tears. He was a good-looking twenty-five-year-old in need of a shave and a haircut. He was trying to appear tough but did not have the features for convincing meanness and simply looked sullen at the stranger's having interrupted his time out for a smoke.

"The feller that drove the buckboard through this gateway," the half-breed answered, and gestured with a movement of his head to indicate the clear tracks of hooves and wheel rims that overprinted the other sign in the dust.

They were tracks that he had seen time and time again between Wildwood and San Sarita, but never more clearly, it seemed to Edge, than during the few minutes since he rode into town. This was a town in which not a great deal happened in the blistering heat of afternoon. Certainly there was not much coming and going on the open streets and the plaza. Thus it had been easy to follow the tracks of Luis Garcia's buckboard over the final few yards of its long journey, down the street and across the plaza to the front of El Estelar Cantina. Then from there, after the horse in the traces had had time to deposit a heap of apples, the rig was set rolling toward and through the post gateway. Once inside, it was driven around the left side to the rear of the former mansion.

All this had been plainly seen by a man with a bad headache that seemed to be caused by the action of his brain trying to outgrow the confines of his skull. The ache had taken a harsher hold within sight of San Sarita, and Edge's idea about why it was recurring had become more firmly entrenched with every slow-moving stride of the gelding carrying him closer to this squalid community where he knew the tracks ended.

"I think you do not want to see him, *gringo*," the corporal with the finely honed features responded, and was fleetingly afraid as he saw the scowl on the face of the half-breed. The man's right hand moved toward the flapped holster on his hip and his dark eyes flicked along their sockets to look, Edge guessed, toward the rifle the corporal had abandoned when he heard the clop of hooves approaching the post entrance.

"I figure you have a good reason to argue the point, kid," the half-breed countered evenly, and made a conscious effort to bring something close to the usual impassiveness to his face.

The corporal dropped the hand away from his holster and forgot about the rifle as he nodded vigorously and explained, "*Sí, sí, señor*. I think you seek the *hombre* who drives the *carro* to San Sarita?"

Edge needed to raise a hand up from the saddlehorn to press the tips of his fingers against the center of his forehead, the place where his swollen brain felt most painfully likely to burst out into the open. The gesture helped a little, and as the pressure subsided, the information given him by the sloppily dressed Federale registered.

"You hit the nail on the head, kid," he said, and tried what could have been a grin in what he felt was a necessary attempt to mask the bad shape he was in.

"*Bueno, señor*. It was my brother Ramón who brings the *carro* to the post. He is Sargento Ramón Lopez, and I cannot see how a *gringo* such as you could have the business with—"

"Your brother's a gambling man, huh?" Edge cut in, and suddenly felt more weary than in pain as his punished brain transmitted to his travel-tired frame the prospect of trailing Delmar Pyle over countless more miles.

"En efecto, señor!" the corporal said enthusiastically. "In the dice shooting in the cantina Ramón wins the *carro* and the *caballo*. If you wish, señor, I will wake my brother so that he can say I tell the truth. But he will not be in a good humor. He will have the hangover. There was much drinking in the celebration of—"

"Happy to have your brother sleep it off, kid. Unless he happens to know where the feller who lost went to after—"

"I can tell you that, señor."

The threat of exhaustion receded and the pain began to throb again, but Edge managed to confine his visible response to an inquiring glint in his hooded, narrowed eyes.

"The *gringo* lost everything, señor," the corporal supplied, eager to please. "Not just to Ramón. Jaime Carrillo won his guns, and his money was divided among many of the . . ." He saw a hardening of the half-breed's expression and hurried on. "He was invited to join in the celebration, señor. He drink much. More than anyone else, I think. *Matar el gusanillo?*"

The good-looking young non-com shifted his uneasy gaze away from the sweating, heavily bristled face of Edge to direct a glance toward the cantina on the east side of the plaza.

"You telling me Delmar Pyle is still here in San Sarita, kid?"

A nod. *"Sí, señor.* I have not been as watchful as a *centinela* should be, I know. There is not the point. Little happens in San Sarita. But he has no money. No *caballo.* Where could he go? Look, you ask Manuel

138

Martinez, who is playing the cards over there. He owns El Estelar Cantina. He can say for sure if the *gringo* who lost all he had is still—''

''Much obliged, Corporal'' Edge cut in on the fast-talking young man and swung down out of the saddle. He led the gelding by the reins on a catty-cornered line across the plaza, bypassing the cottonwoods under which the merchants were gathered to go directly to the front of the cantina. And as he did so, he spared a glance back up the street by which he had entered town and out along the open trail. He saw no sign yet of the flatbed wagon and the buggy against the heat haze that would soon begin to lift as the afternoon drew toward evening.

In Mexican, the Federale on sentry duty at the gateway of the post called to the men under the cotton-woods that he was sure there was going to be trouble at the cantina, but the card game on the bench had already been interrupted as the men recognized the menacing way the half-breed moved toward his objective.

The spokesman of the group said in American, ''I think he has some Mexican in him. In his blood and in his understanding of what is said.''

''Half my blood, feller,'' Edge called out as he hitched the reins of the gelding to one of a row of rings hanging on the cantina wall. ''And every word my pa knew.''

''But you prefer to speak the language of the *gringos*. So I will address you so. To tell you that Manuel Martinez welcomes anybody to his cantina. Unless there is the *intención* to cause trouble.''

Edge's head continued to pound, but he tried to ignore it. He glanced across at the stand of cottonwoods and saw that the six men had risen off the benches and now stood in a line, all of them apparently unarmed. Nonetheless there was a quality of menace in the way they stood and looked at him. He knew though, that there was potentially greater danger from within the cantina, for despite what the young Federale had said about Delmar Pyle losing his revolver in a crap game, there was still the strong possibility he had rearmed himself.

Something small and light was tossed out through the doorway to drop into the dust at his feet. He looked down at it suspiciously, and immediately wrenched his head around when the man he had come to kill said, "only thing of yours I got left, mister." Then he belched and followed this with what sounded like a giggle. "Edge, I give you back the edge."

It was the razor stolen from his neck pouch that lay in the dust just outside the cantina threshold. As he went down on his haunches and located the razor by feel, the half-breed continued to peer in through the doorway at where the indistinct form of the only customer could be seen in the shadowy gloom of late afternoon. Pyle giggled more plainly as Edge straightened up, but then he broke down into the more familiar sobs that Edge had heard at Dry River Valley.

"Please, mister. Please don't hurt me. If you don't hurt me, I'll see you get—"

"He is unarmed, señor," Martinez said from behind Edge as the man in the cantina was forced to break off his entreaties by an uncontrollable assault of self-pity and dread. "And has drunk much. I beg of you, do not—"

"No sweat," the half-breed broke in as he pushed the razor into his neck pouch and swung through the doorway. Speaking only loud enough for the man inside to hear him, he added, "All I'm fixing to kill for a while is some time."

"Thank God," Pyle groaned.

"Until the Newton woman gets here."

The man at the table, who was dressed in a shirt and necktie and the vest and pants of a once well-styled suit, tried to get to his feet. But his legs threatened to collapse under him and his head rocked from side to side. He dropped hard down onto the chair again and vented another foolish giggle.

"Aside from that, you ain't ready."

"Huh?" Then Pyle gave another belch.

Edge back-heeled the door violently closed and drawled, "Heard it said a drunken man feels no pain."

Chapter Twelve

DELMAR PYLE said to Edge as hooves and wheels were heard coming down the street from the north, "I know it sounds crazy, and I guess it is a kinda madness, mister, but the kinda gambling streak I got in me is like a disease that there ain't nothing can be done to cure. An incurable disease, that's what it is for sure."

Edge dropped a cigarette butt on the floor and ground it into a mess of paper and cold tobacco beneath his heel. He nodded in agreement and said, "Figure it's going to be the death of you, feller."

"But you ain't heard that deal I've got in mind yet, Edge."

Twilight had been falling over northern Sonora some thirty minutes earlier as the half-breed was entering El Estelar Cantina and sat at the same table as Pyle. It was a corner table and the shorter, younger man with the blue-green eyes and very white teeth sat with his back to the rear wall. Edge had lowered himself gratefully onto the chair that was backed to the side wall so that Pyle was within arm's reach on his left and Edge had a clear view over the room, with its door and two windows at the front and an archway in back of the counter that ran halfway along the rear wall. The place was not as large as the cantina at Wildwood and there were just six tables crowding its floor area, but Manuel Martinez ran a neater, cleaner establishment than had Marshall Troy. Martinez had cleaned up whatever mess had been made during the crap-shooting session and the drinking jag that followed it. Except, that is, for the liquored-up and passed out Delmar Pyle who now, Edge had to allow, looked in a whole lot better shape than he did himself.

The door the half-breed had kicked closed was opened again as he took the chair at Pyle's table. It was the sixty-year-old, round-faced, fleshy Martinez who entered and left the door standing wide open as he crossed to go behind the bar counter, where he lit two kerosene lamps that dropped soft cones of light to drive back the murk of evening and give the bottles on the shelves behind the counter a tantalizing gleam. Only then, as he took up an arms-akimbo attitude behind the counter, did Martinez announce resolutely, "This is my place, señor. It is night, so I light the lamps. It is hot and I am open for the business, so the door stays open."

"Since it is your place, no sweat," Edge answered evenly as he completed rolling the cigarette that had occupied him since he took his seat.

"Sin animo de ofender, señor," the owner of the place countered, and pointedly wrinkled his nose. "For I can tell you have traveled far. But because you sweat is yet another reason for the door to be open."

"No offense taken, feller. I know it." He struck a

match on the butt of the ancient revolver taken from the dead Calvin Terry. As he lit the cigarette, his slitted eyes glittered menacingly in its flare as he gazed coldly at Pyle.

"I know, I know," the frightened man said hurriedly, nodding his head vigorously. "It's all my fault you've had such a hard time, but I can make up for it, mister. I can cut you in on a deal that'll make you richer than Cornelius Vanderbilt."

Edge took off his hat and set it, brim down, on the center of the table. "Last time we had anything to say to each other, feller, I got a headache. Still have it, and maybe that means my brain's damaged. But it ain't addled so much—"

Pyle shook his head this time, directed a suspicious glance toward Martinez, and raised a hand to shield his lips from the scowling owner of the cantina to whisper as he leaned closer to Edge, "A lost gold mine, mister. Sunk into the richest seam in the whole of the Sierra Madre."

Martinez cleared his throat irritably, and splayed his hands on the counter top. "Is it just my table and chairs you wish to use for free? Or maybe I can get you food and drink? Sometimes I get the customers in my cantina for such things!"

"You know I'm flat busted," Pyle responded to the sarcasm, a grimace on his face and bitterness in his tone.

"Coffee and a couple of enchiladas, feller," Edge said. "But only if you'll accept my horse as collateral."

"And I get paid cash money when this *hombre*'s *ensueño* come true, huh?" Martinez sneered.

"My what?" Pyle asked, his confidence growing by the moment as the effects of the liquor wore off.

145

"Daydream," Edge supplied.

"The hell it is!" Pyle blurted. "Just wait until Captain Gomez gets back to the post and I get in to see—"

Pyle elected to cut short his rebuttal without outside pressure. And from the way he swept a suspicious glance from Martinez to the open door and back again, it was apparent he feared he had already said too much. But only cool evening air and aromas of cooking and the sounds of passing footfalls came over the threshold while the man behind the bar counter waited expectantly for a response to his question.

"Woman coming down the trail from Wildwood, feller. I'm working for her and due a payday. Ain't sure she has any cash with her, but she's got a wagon and team and some goods aboard the wagon."

"Just one woman, Edge?" Pyle asked, apprehensive again. "Yeah, you made mention of just the Newton da—"

"Shut up, feller," Edge told him evenly on a stream of tobacco smoke while he continued to look toward Martinez. "If she's got no money and money's all you'll take, *patrón*, Felipe Chevez will vouch she's good for it. You know him?"

"*Sí*, I know the priest from Wildwood, señor," the Mexican answered, his attitude suddenly less hostile. He even showed an expectant smile when he asked, "Father Chevez is coming to town tonight?"

"Any time now. With the lady who'll pay my way and the *Viuda* Banales."

Martinez expressed shock. "Pablo Banales is dead, señor?"

Pyle swallowed hard.

"It happens to everybody sooner or later," Edge said.

Martinez came out from behind his counter and gestured with both pudgy hands to signal dismissal of what Edge had said. "That is coffee and enchiladas. I can fill such an order, señor, but Conchita Romanos who works for my *amigo* Fernando Ruiz at the restaurant is much better at the *arte culinario*. And I am eager to tell that Father Chevez is coming to town. He is such a fine man. You will pardon my absence? If you require something stronger than coffee before I return, *sirvase usted*, eh?"

He moved toward the doorway as he spoke with rising excitement. Then he came to an impatient halt on the threshold when the half-breed called, *"Patrón?"*

"Sí, señor?"

"I'm just loaning you my horse until the lady reaches town. Be obliged if you'd have him attended to. Tell the liveryman he'll be paid. Same arrangement as for your friend Ruiz if you can swing it."

"No es molestia, señor," the Mexican assured him before he turned to hurry out the cantina doorway.

"I bet he said you got nothing to worry about, mister?" Pyle growled with a baleful look toward the empty threshold and that part of the moonlit plaza that was visible beyond. Edge nodded. "Yeah," Pyle said in the same tone. "Around here they all think the sun shines outa that priest's asshole, Edge, on account of most of the loot he wins off the guys that go to Wildwood for the games of chance he brings down here to San Sarita to spread around the deadbeats."

"Nothing wrong with charity, feller."

"A guy's supposed to give to it, not have some card-sharping priest take him to the cleaners." Pyle shot a glance at the doorway to make sure Martinez was not on his way back inside before he spat on the hard-packed dirt of the floor.

"I heard he took you for some of the money you stole off me, feller."

Pyle looked sharply at Edge, seeking any sign of anger. Seeing only the half-breed's usual neutral expression, Pyle continued the discussion. "One day I'm gonna prove a guy can't be a loser all his damn life, Edge."

The half-breed seemed to be gazing into infinity and was totally detached from the cantina when he murmured, "I know the feeling, feller."

Pyle was confused a moment. Then he decided to read what was best for him into the remark. "Hey, I figured you and me had somethin' in common, mister. And I should've realized you showed me a sign when you give the order for coffee and two enchiladas, huh?"

"I'm two enchiladas hungry is why."

"Shit, thanks for nothin', mister!"

"Always seemed to me a waste of good grub to feed a condemened man."

"Shit," Pyle rasped again, then darted out his tongue to flick it between his lips before he asked obsequiously, "How about takin' up Martinez on his offer of a drink?"

"Had a couple of snorts of tequila at the wake Calvin Terry was holding for his partner And I figure that's what started my head to hurting again."

"And you ain't gonna stand no treat for me?" Pyle snarled.

"What you're owed by me is nothing like a free drink, feller."

"That from a guy that says there ain't nothin' wrong with charity!" This time he didn't take the time to check the doorway before he spat at the floor.

"Don't they say that begins at home? I live under my hat, and right now I'm not wearing mine."

Delmar Pyle glowered malevolently at his table companion for long seconds, but then realized the emotional resources this required were wasted on a man set to ignore anything that was not of striking interest to him. For a minute or so after Pyle reached this conclusion, both men showed nothing of what they were thinking as they sat in the fringe glow of the lamps above the bar counter, smelling cooking food that was now strong enough to mask the stinks of their own unwashed bodies and listening to the hum of a quiet town when the work of the day was done and suppertime was almost here.

They were still silent when a fat and aged but oddly beautiful woman came into the cantina with a tray covered by a cloth. After setting this down on the table before Edge, she wished him enjoyment of his food and assured him an empty plate would be thanks enough for her trouble.

After the woman left, Delmar Pyle sniffed the aromatic air and eyed the laden tray with the doleful eyes of a hungry animal that is almost certain it will not get fed.

"You want to go sit at another table while I'm eating, I won't stop you, feller," the half-breed told him. "Even wait outside if you figure that'll be best."

"Because you know I won't go anyplace," the disconsolate man said bitterly.

Edge began to eat one of the enchiladas, dipping it into the bowl of chili beans. Then he said, "Not a peso to call your own, your guns are gone, and I guess you never did think about the razor as anything more than something to shave with." He washed down the first half of his meal with a long drink of coffee. Then he added, "Hey, feller, maybe there's a shovel some peon left lying around that you could dig a mine with."

"Ain't polite to talk with your mouth full, I was always taught, mister!"

"In my family, that was one of the rules of the house. But it was pretty far down the list. Way below not killing anybody who wasn't trying to kill you and not stealing and not repaying a favor with a crack on the head and not cheating at games of chance. Especially not cheating at games of chance, on account of my pa was a gambling man and—"

"All right, all right!" Pyle cut in testily as he dry-washed his hands. Then he clenched one into a fist and punched the open palm of the other. Having brought his temper under control, he gazed across the lamplit cantina. But if he saw anything of his spartan surroundings he didn't show it, for there was a look of intense concentration on his pleasant-featured, fleshy face that was not merited by the scene before him. "I was just gonna say I'd like to explain things, since you're eating and I ain't gonna get any food. And, like you said, there's time to kill."

There was no inflection in his voice that suggested he was posing a question, and he did not shift his gaze from the limbo into which he was looking to even glance inquiringly at Edge. But there was a tacit invitation for the half-breed to fill the pause, and when he did not, Pyle placed a positive interpretation on the silence. Against the subdued sounds of the half-breed's horse being unhitched from the ring beyond the open doorway and led toward the livery stable, Delmar Pyle began:

"Never knew your pa, so I can't be sure about it, mister. But I'd guess he wasn't bit by the gambling bug worse than me. I just can't help myself. If I ain't gambling, I ain't living, not really. Win or lose, it's all the same.'' He spoke in a dull monotone, but there was a look of high excitement in his expression for a few moments, as if he was engaged in a game of chance right now. Which, Edge reflected, maybe he was. Then he continued, deeply concentrating again, ''Trouble with gambling, though—one of the troubles—is that the man that really needs credit ain't the one to get it. Only the rich get it. Until the bank opens or they sell some stocks or remortgage the house. The likes of me . . .''

He shrugged and sighed bitterly. ''But things are gonna be different soon, mister. I won me a half share in a lost gold mine that I just know is gonna make me a rich man. Guy who owned it put it up against a thousand-buck ante, mister. Said it was worth a thousand times that, but it was all he had left to bet with. And my little flush beat his high straight. Right there and then—up in El Paso a year or so ago—I needed a grand in cash more than I needed any piece of paper that gave me title to a gold mine. But the guy that lost to me got himself killed in a gunfight before he had the chance to buy his marker back.''

''You're telling me something I already heard, feller,'' Edge broke in after he finished the final mouthful of his supper and took out the makings. ''Except I heard it was in a saloon brawl he was killed.''

''A brawl got started sure enough, mister, but only after he broke into the safe and left it open with plenty of money inside because he took just the thousand dollars he needed to buy back the marker I was holding. And, I tell you, he wasn't no safecracker nor robber of any kind by nature. He was just desperate to get back that paper for a half share of the mine.''

"Which you've been holding for more than a year since then," Edge responded as Pyle looked at him with round, beseeching eyes.

Pyle made to start dry-washing his hands again, but then hooked them over the rim of the table and pressed down hard to keep them from shaking. He nodded. "I know, I know. But this lousy gambling bug I got eating away at me all the time . . . I stayed lucky in El Paso. Heard about some high rolling up in Santa Fe. From there I drifted across to Tucson. There was a woman in that town took me for everything I had, the bitch. Picked up a stake in Tombstone. But it weren't much more than eating money. More important, I heard a rumor there. I heard that a guy named Sam Colville had struck it rich down over the border in Sonora. I already know that a guy of that name held the paper on the other half of the lost gold mine, mister."

Both his voice and his face revealed remembered excitement, and behind his impassive expression as he lit the fresh-made cigarette, the half-breed began to nurture a glimmer of interest in the story being told him. For a moment the story was interrupted while Conchita Romanos bustled into the cantina to gather up the dirty dishes. She said she was happy Edge had enjoyed the food, but it was obvious the empty plate and bowl and cup were not the sole cause of the beaming joy on the old woman's beautiful face.

Today, she explained in fast-spoken Mexican, was the birthday of Father Felipe Chevez, and since he was coming to San Sarita, everyone in town had an opportunity to repay him, in part at least, for all the good he had done. Every able-bodied citizen was busy in the preparation for a fine feast that was to be held in his honor in the restaurant of Fernando Ruiz.

"Heard the priest's name and saw how the old biddy was grinning from ear to ear," Pyle growled sourly after Conchita Romanos left. "Him and the others been spotted heading into town?"

"She didn't say so. It's his birthday. Whole town's going to throw a party for him."

His scowl deepened. "Reckon I oughtta get an invite to that, mister. A lot of the dough he's spread around the poor of San Sarita has been won off me. For a guy that wears the white collar the way he does, that priest sure does have the luck of the devil at cards."

"But I guess he doesn't cheat, feller."

"Only when I'm so frigging desperate there ain't no other way!" Pyle defended himself, his temper rising. He gripped the table tightly again and took a few moments to deep-breathe his way back to a precarious degree of self-control. "And I wasn't that desperate for a long time, Edge." His blue-green eyes implored belief again. "I only fooled with the rules against guys that were fixing to get sharp with me. And that didn't happen in Wildwood. The games were straight and I hit a losing streak. All I had left was the paper that gave me a half share in the mine. But I had that safe in Luis Garcia's bank. I wasn't gonna risk losing that when I was so close to Hopeville. Which is where the claim is. Real close to Hopeville anyway, is what I was told. Whole lot of claims staked in that piece of country, and guys that staked them are hitting paydirt. Enough of them came north to Wildwood for the whoring and the gambling and paid with dust and nuggets to show there's rich pickings to be had."

"But you just couldn't tear yourself away from the action at Marshall Troy's place to check out your claim, huh?" Edge growled.

All at once they heard the clatter of rigs approaching on the street that ran toward the plaza from the north.

"I know it sounds crazy," Pyle said. "And I guess it is a kinda madness, mister, but the kinda gambling streak I got in me is like a disease that there ain't nothing can be done to cure. An incurable disease, that's what it is for sure."

"Figure it's going to be the death of you, feller."

"But you ain't heard that deal I've got in mind yet, Edge."

The half-breed put his hat back on his head, which ached hardly at all now, and ground the mess of the cigarette butt even harder into the dirt as he rose from the table. He said, "That the one that's going to make me as rich as Vanderbilt, feller? But I don't have to fool around with railroads and shipping lines and stuff like that, eh? Just have to get me a shovel and dig a hole in the ground." He started toward the doorway that opened onto the plaza, but paused to show Delmar Pyle a grim smile that caused the seated man to grip the table even more tightly. Then he drawled, "Last time I did that, it was poor I finished up, not rich."

The man at the corner table was tensed up to counter Edge's irony, but he found he was unable to give sound to the words he wanted to speak until after the lean, darkly bristled, mirthlessly smiling, glittering-eyed face was turned away from him and the half-breed had reached the doorway, where he came to a halt. The half-breed assumed a nonchalant attitude with his back to the frame so that he could as easily look into the cantina as across the plaza or along the street that ran down from the north trail.

"Anyone close enough out there to hear what I'm sayin'?"

Edge took the trouble to scan the plaza, which was lit by the moon over most of its area, while lamplight from most of the surrounding buildings reached far enough to dispel the shadows from beneath the cottonwoods at the center.

"Nobody, feller," he reported truthfully, for with the exception of Cabo Lopez, who now stood visibly at sentry duty inside the gates of the Federale post, there was no one in sight except for the eager group out front of the restaurant directly across the plaza from the cantina. The group emanated a near palpable aura of excitement as all faces turned smilingly to peer at the advancing buggy with the flatbed wagon rolling behind it.

"Sam Colville is a prisoner of the Federale captain who runs the San Sarita post," Delmar Pyle said urgently in a rasping whisper that reached across the empty cantina. "I was down to nothing but the paper on the mine when I found that out from the priest after one of his trips down here. Of course, he just made mention of it in passing. It was part of the gossip. Nobody but me knew he was the other partner in the mine—and the only partner to have, since he knows where to dig to hit right into that rich seam.

"Gomez wants a thousand bucks to turn Colville loose, and I didn't have a lousy cent. I was desperate then, mister. But you don't do nothing funny with Wildwood folks. Far as money's concerned, you don't. I asked Garcia for a loan from the bank, but I wasn't about to tell him what for, and he wouldn't give me no loan. Got me the job fetching and carrying for them two women out on the Dry River Valley place. Took it hoping they had some money around the place, seeing as how they was going into business. But they kept it all in the bank. I was biding my time, saving cash for the first time in my life, I guess. Getting together enough to get me in a big game, the kind where, Wildwood or not, I'd be willing to risk a little sharping after I was sure I could make a run across the border if I was caught out.

"But that McCall dame, she just ain't sold on the same woman-to-woman stuff as the other one, mister. And like everything else I'm telling you, it's the truth that I could've had her most any day since I started to work out at their place if the Newton dame hadn't been around. She used to sashay about the place real provocative when she knew I was eyeing her and her buddy wasn't."

Pyle increased the speed of his talk as they heard the two rigs approaching the plaza, but he didn't raise his voice, and so Edge moved off the threshold and across the cantina to stand with a hip leaning on the bar counter. The seated man nodded several times as he continued to account for his motives, apparently encouraged by the fact that his listener wanted to hear everything clearly.

"Yesterday morning was too much, mister. And you know the rest of what happened at their place. The temptation of getting away from there with all I could take from them and you was just too much. But then I found a game going on at Troy's place in Wildwood, and I figured my luck had changed." He spat at the usual place on the dirt floor. "Some friggin' hope! And when it got to the crucial point, I didn't have the guts to do no sharpin' in that company. Then I got scared about you and them two women comin' after me. Found my luck wasn't all out, because Garcia was comin' across the border to see the Banales couple and so I got a ride with him. Didn't have no idea he was bringin' cash money to loan those people, and when I saw that foldin' green, mister, I got tempted a different way.''

A chorus of voices was raised to welcome Father Chevez, and as the sound spread across the plaza and reached into the cantina, it spurred Delmar Pyle to talk even faster.

''I hadn't never killed no one before. You can believe that or not, don't make no difference. But it was easy. I just grabbed old man Banales' shotgun and let him and Garcia have it. The old lady ran out the back—to get another gun, I figured. I didn't have no more shells and I ain't much with a pistol or a rifle, so I just hightailed it away from there on Garcia's buckboard.''

The buggy and the wagon had come to a standstill on the far side of the plaza while the noisy welcoming of the priest rose to a crescendo. But when the barrage of joyful sound began to subside, the clop of hooves could still be heard without the accompanying clatter of turning wheels. The sound of a horse and rider was approaching town on the trail from the south.

''I said you could shift while I was eating,'' Edge growled when Pyle made to rise from the table.

''Just wanna see if that's Gomez coming back to town.'' He remained standing behind the table but leaned to the side to get a better view through the doorway, then sat down with a scowl, for the clump of cottonwoods masked the end of the street across the plaza.

''You're broke, feller,'' the half-breed said as he moved away from the bar counter back to the doorway. ''You told me. Like you told me too, it's going to take a thousand dollars to spring your partner from the local jug.''

From the doorway, Edge saw first that the wrought-iron gates of the Federale post had been opened and that there was a four-man guard on duty. The other three sentries were as sloppily dressed as the corporal, but all were standing at rigid attention with their rifles at the port. Then he saw four more uniformed men as they slowed their mounts from a trot to a walk when they rode onto the plaza. There were an officer, a sergeant, and two corporals. Next he shifted his unblinking gaze to where Harriet Newton was talking with the owner of the cantina, the two of them standing beside the wagon a little apart from the main body of people crowded around the buggy.

"Is it him?" Pyle insisted.

"An officer and three non-coms."

"Gomez is the only officer at San Sarita."

Comandante Gomez was a man of about forty, stockily built with a round face in which his eyes were too small and his mouth too wide. He looked weary with life rather than just from the ride, which had evidently been a long one, from the state of the horses. But innate character or military training caused him to maintain an arrogant erect posture in his saddle as he surveyed the plaza. His tiny eyes swept the scene just once before he led the way through the gates of the post, but Edge felt certain the Federale officer had missed nothing.

Not the half-breed silhouetted in the doorway against the lamplight. Not Harriet Newton who came toward the cantina, directed by the raised and pointing hand of Manuel Martinez. Not the subtle atmosphere generated by the now extremely quiet crowd of people before the restaurant, an atmosphere that held a strange quality of menace mixed with melancholy, the menace created by resentment that the melancholy came so suddenly in the wake of joyousness.

"Thanks for waiting, Edge," the redheaded woman said as she closed with the half-breed. Her voice was dull and her thin face and slender body looked more spare than he remembered. "I wasn't sure you would."

He moved aside so she could step inside the cantina, and she gasped and almost stumbled when she saw Delmar Pyle.

"Miss Newton, I—" he started to say in a strangled tone as he half rose again.

The woman came to a halt and threw up both her hands to press them to her ears. Her green eyes widened and filled with an intensity of emotion summoned from a reserve that a moment before had seemed exhausted. The hate that blazed in her eyes sharpened the shrillness of her voice to a near painful degree when she shrieked, "Now! Do it now! Blast the murdering bastard to eternity!"

"Please!" Pyle groaned, tears súddenly spilling down his cheeks. He hurled aside the table as he dropped off the chair and onto his knees. He clasped his hands together to complete the attitude of prayer. "No!"

Outside the cantina the negative seemed to be taken up in a variety of Mexican and American pleas and demands that the woman's order should not be obeyed. The babble of urgent voices exploded across the plaza from the throng of San Sarita citizens who began to surge forward, translating latent menace into threatening action.

A gunshot sounded, not exceptionally loud amid the clamor of voices, but the implication of the sound had the effect of shocking the crowd into tense, brittle silence. Harriet Newton wrenched her bright-eyed gaze away from the beseeching form of Delmar Pyle and

159

snarled at Edge, "You missed him, you crazy son of a bitch! You frigging missed—"

She broke off when she realized that the revolver the half-breed had taken off a dead man was still in the holster. And utter perplexity displaced the rage that had begun to distort her face to ugliness.

Edge had not seen the earlier expression, for he had been turned from the waist to watch as the crowd became silent and still in response to the firing of the revolver by Comandante Gomez, who now moved out through the post gateway, brought the gun down from its angle at the night sky, and pushed it back into his hip holster. There was as much arrogance in the way he did this and in his upright gait as there had been in the way he sat in the saddle.

"You said you were gonna . . ."

The redhead looked and sounded emotionally and physically drained again as Pyle toppled onto his side, curled up into a tight ball, and sobbed into his cupped hands.

Edge nodded and drawled, "Yeah, lady. Said it and meant it. But I can only aim to please when I don't get beat to the draw."

Chapter Thirteen

THE FEDERALE officer halted before the cantina doorway and leaned a little to one side to direct a glance between Edge on the threshold and the redhead just beyond to see the curled-up form of the hapless Delmar Pyle. Then he threw up a curt salute and followed this with a bow that was like a habitual reflex action. He said, "*Buenas tardes, señorita, señor.* I am Antonio Gomez. Captain Gomez. The comandante of the Federale post here in San Sarita. I have traveled far today on government business and have much need for refreshment. I trust you will permit me to enter the cantina of my friend Manuel Martinez? And then, perhaps you will do me the honor of sharing a bottle of wine with me?"

Pyle got a tentative grip on his composure while Gomez was speaking, the Mexican's manner as mockingly polite as the salute and the bow had been. And from the townspeople, who were no longer in such a close-knit group—they were spread across a large area of the plaza between the cottonwoods and the restaurant—there emanated yet another growling sound of hostility toward Gomez. The grimace on the face of the cantina owner as he came toward his place showed clearly he was as unfavorably disposed toward the Federale officer as were his fellow citizens. Harriet Newton simply gazed with a kind of jaded sadness at Edge, who could not be certain he was successful in his efforts to conceal ice-cold anger behind impassivity.

Edge stepped back so that Gomez and then the owner could enter the cantina ahead of him.

"There are certain acts that even a man of my power in this town cannot command, señor," Gomez responded as the redhead backed out of his path, bumped a chair, and sank wearily into it. "If you will not take a drink with me, you will not."

Pyle had got unsteadily to his feet, wiping shirt-sleeves across his tear-reddened eyes. Then he tried a smile as he blurted, "You don't have to ask me twice, Comandante. Way I was brought up, it ain't polite to refuse an offer—"

"Brought up in the way of vomit?" the officer broke in as he reached the bar counter and turned to lean against it. With an expression of supreme self-assurance, he pushed his elbows backward far enough so they rested on the top. "Which is sometimes what I feel like doing when I see a fully grown man weeping, unless he weeps from grief for a loved one. Perhaps there is one who would have wept for you had I not intervened just now?" He shook his head and showed a mocking frown. "It is difficult to imagine, I think."

Obviously filling the man's usual order, Manuel Martinez went immediately behind the bar counter and stooped to bring a bottle of wine from beneath. He set a glass close to where the Federale leaned, and glowered at the man's broad back as he worked with a corkscrew to open the bottle.

Pyle sat down on the same chair as before, staring down at the backs of his hands as his fingers clawed at his thighs.

"Is everybody sure?" Gomez asked when he heard the wine being poured. "It is fine, from France. Not the filthy stuff that is made in this area."

"All I want, mister, is to see that creep dead," Harriet Newton said with a deep sigh that suggested what she wanted was a lost cause.

Martinez, tidy minded despite the circumstances and his frustration, set upright the table Pyle had overturned and with a scowl toward Edge at the doorway gathered up the shreds of the two cigarettes the half-breed had ground into the dirt floor.

"If there is just cause for this to happen, señorita," Gomez said in a less ironic tone as he swung around to face the bar, "then it may still be so. But you must understand my position here in San Sarita. You are in Mexico now, and I am the highest representative of my government here." He briefly became authoritative as he barked a command in his native language for Martinez to leave the cantina and close the door behind him on his way out. While the owner of the place complied, partly angry to be ordered off his own premises and partly relieved to be able to go, the Federale officer sat at a table between those of Pyle and the woman. He took the bottle with him and did not have his first sip of the rich red wine until he was seated. Then, when the door closed, the uniformed Mexican leaned back in his chair and reverted to American. "My position, in such a town as this, is not—how shall I say . . . ?"

"Inflexible, feller," Edge said evenly as he leaned against the wall beside the closed door and dug the makings from his shirt pocket.

A nod and a smile. "That is it precisely. A man must bend with the way the wind blows."

"And it's a real ill one if it doesn't blow you some good, feller."

Gomez inclined his head again. "I am a fine student of the American language, señor. I know this expression and I allow that it applies to me." He shrugged shortly. "The outpost here is not a prime one. A man must use his position to make the best of—"

"I heard it's gonna take a thousand American dollars to get Sam Colville out of your prison, Comandante," Pyle blurted as he stared down at his hands clutching his thighs. Then he snapped up his head to watch for a reaction, expecting the worst.

And Harriet Newton vented a snort of disgust that was probably about as mannish a sound as she ever got to utter.

The small eyes in the round face glinted from out of the shadow of the Federale's cap visor. But the depth of feeling they expressed was no match for the casual smile that set the line of his too-wide mouth. Then he took another sip of the wine and said with a quality of nonchalance rather than the avarice that showed in his eyes, "If such a rumor proved to be correct, señor, you could afford to pay such a price to secure the release of the prisoner?"

Pyle swallowed hard and the grimace that crossed his fleshy face suggested it was something more palpable than a mixture of eagerness and disappointment that he gulped down his throat.

"He had it," Edge supplied while the man at the

table in the corner of the cantina struggled to keep the bile out of his mouth. "In cash and kind, I figure."

"What kind of kind?" Gomez asked, and the smile on his lips became one of quiet satisfaction as he relished his successful play on words in a language not his own.

"In cash and nuggets I had it all," Pyle said quickly, his blue-green eyes flicking quickly back and forth between the Mexican and the man who was half Mexican. Perhaps he had forgotten about the woman who sat at the table close to where the half-breed stood at the closed door. Or maybe he had to make a considerable effort to avoid looking toward her and seeing the depth of the malevolence she directed at him.

"The cash was from Luis Garcia after you murdered him and the farmer," the redhead said in ice-cold tones that forced Pyle to meet her gaze. "You got the gold after you killed Curtis Webster."

She and the man she hated so deeply both switched their attention to Gomez as Edge struck a match on the wall to light his cigarette. Each of them was eager to see how the man responsible for law and order in this area of Sonora reacted to the revelations of murder.

"I know of the banker from Wildwood," Gomez said, no longer smiling, but neither was he grim faced. "I saw Señora Banales ride to town with the Wildwood priest. Her husband is the farmer of who—"

"It was an accident!" Pyle snarled, and found emotional reserves to power a challenging scowl at Edge and Harriet Newton. "A misunderstandin'."

"The same with the prospector?" the woman sneered.

"No! The son of a bitch tried to cheat at cards! I don't care what the guy that was his partner told you! He was helping Webster cheat me! I oughtta have blasted him to hell the same as the other one! Tried to, dammit, but he beat it down into the tunnels! And I wasn't about to take off after him, seeing as how he knew the layout and I didn't. Just took the whole pot that was left from the game. It was my due after the bastards tried to cheat on me. Same as I took the money Garcia was gonna give to Banales. They tried to kill me first. I can explain all that in detail if you wanna hear it, Comandante.''

Gomez had finished his first glass of wine and was pouring another while Delmar Pyle was blurting out his defense.

''I know of the tenses in your language, señor,'' the Federale said before Harriet Newton could give sound to the first word of the denial her mouth had formed. ''You *had* the thousand dollars. You stated it thus. As did you.'' He gestured toward Edge with his glass and his eyes.

Pyle was briefly content with the way his explanation had been so calmly accepted, but now was disheartened again. ''A bunch of your men have it, Comandante. All of it. And the horse and buckboard I drove to San Sarita on.''

''All my men have it?''

''He's a gambling fool, Captain,'' Edge supplied.

''A born loser who just won't admit that's what he is,'' the woman added in much the same even tone as the half-breed.

Gomez sipped some wine and shook his head slowly. His expression was now as impassive as that of Edge, but his tone of voice revealed he was experiencing a mild degree of disappointment. ''It seems that on this occasion the ill wind has blown the good to some of my men, eh?''

Pyle shook his head much more vigorously and thrust a hand into his hip pocket as he came to his feet fast. "Look, we can all be winners! Big winners!"

Gomez streaked a hand to the flap of his holster and Harriet Newton reached to draw the Remington that was gone from hers. Then both saw it was just a folded sheet of dirty and creased paper Pyle produced from his back pocket.

"Lost his weapons too," Edge said.

The woman sighed and the Federale rasped, *"Hijo de puta!"*

The redhead moved her hand from the empty holster to her throat while she considered that she might have been killed by Delmar Pyle. The uniformed man took a deep swallow of wine, reflecting, Edge guessed, on just how frightened the Mexican had been in those moments when he was certain the fast-moving man was about to draw a gun.

"Look, I'm flat busted and in the worst straits I've ever been in, you people," Pyle pleaded, and his whole being begged that he be listened to as he gingerly unfolded the paper while he constantly swept his gaze over the faces of each member of his small audience. He made just one more small tear in the paper before it was opened up and he held it out at arm's length. "I sure ain't never gambled with this before. It's a half share in the richest strike in the Sierra Madre. And I'm putting up three-quarters of it. A quarter goes to each of you people, and if each of you cover my bet, we'll all be rich. And maybe you all can be double rich if you can get Sam Colville to . . . Hey, you ain't heard me out!"

Desperation came close to panic as Gomez pushed back his chair and stood up.

"For all these riches, señor, you require from me simply the release of Samuel Colville?" the Federale asked. And now there was the hint of humor in his glinting eyes while his mouth line remained solemn.

"Yeah, that's right. And from these others I just want them to forget they figure they got reason to want me dead."

Delmar Pyle's pleading look drew no response from the redhead and the half-breed.

"Señorita, señor," Gomez said as he moved toward the door, "I intend to release the prisoner as has been requested. If you do not also do what has been asked of you during the next few minutes, you will regret the consequences. I make myself understood?"

He had opened the door and now paused on the threshold to flick a questioning gaze between Edge and Harriet Newton.

"I could kill a rat in cold blood, Captain," the woman said bitterly. "But I can't kill one in human form that way."

"I can be a fool sometimes, feller," Edge replied. "But this isn't one of them."

"*Bueno*." Gomez brightened the smile and shared it among the three people he left in the lamplit cantina before he swung out through the doorway.

Only Pyle responded with a brief, weary smile of his own as he sat down again and held the tattered sheet of paper in both hands, to reread perhaps for the thousand and first time what was written upon it.

If Gomez showed his smile to the large throng of people gathered on the moonlit plaza, none of them watched his striding figure with a similar expression. There was anger in the night air; it seemed more tangible than the woodsmoke of forgotten cooking fires. Feet shuffled, bodies swayed, and heads turned. But if there was talk as the mass of eyes followed the strutting officer in through the gateway then switched attention back to the open doorway of the cantina, it could not be distinguished from the faint rustling of the cottonwood foliage in a stray current of air which was all that disturbed the stillness.

"He bought it," Pyle murmured a moment later, and moved the paper up to his face and kissed it. "He bought the deal, didn't he?"

"Guess a born loser is just bound to have plenty of optimism, feller," Edge said.

"There's something I've got plenty of, creep," the redhead said dully, the utter lack of feeling in her voice drawing Pyle's gaze to her stone face. "And that's patience. If you somehow get out of this latest hole you're in and Edge here don't have no more stomach to keep after you . . ." Now a look of spite took ahold of her alluringly unbeautiful face and she spat out the threat as if each word of it was dipped in something that tasted bad. "He ain't the only gun for hire in this neck of the woods!"

"You hired my hate, lady, not my gun," the half-breed said.

"If hate could kill anybody, mister, that creep'd be long dead!" Harriet Newton snarled.

There was a stir of activity out on the plaza and some rasping talk before the angry silence was restored for a moment when the skinny, meagerly bearded Father Felipe Chevez stepped to the front of the press of people and announced in a pulpit tone of voice, "Hatred harms only him who carries it in his heart toward others!"

There was a murmuring of many exchanges as the citizens of San Sarita felt duty-bound to express agreement with what their benefactor had said. Then, the mass conscience appeased, the silence that quivered with angry menace returned to the plaza.

Edge arced the cigarette butt out into the night. It impacted with the hard surface of the plaza in a shower of sparks. As he noticed without concern that Manuel Martinez gave a nod of approval that his floor had not been sullied this time, the half-breed sensed that he should be paying attention to some other far more important aspect of the moonlit scene.

But then he saw all attention swing toward the gateway of the post and decided he had simply been slow to spot the movement beyond. He now saw the Federale officer come around the weed-choked base of the flagpole with another man at his side, a man who would have emphasized by contrast the innate arrogance of Gomez even had he not been dressed only in a set of torn and stained long johns. For he was old and stooped and he staggered like a drunken man though he was not drunk.

The post buildings were sparsely lit and it was not until the two men emerged from the shadows of the wall that they could be seen clearly in the light of the moon and by the illumination that escaped from the windows and doorways of the commercial premises on the plaza. The contrast between the captor and his captive triggered from the watchers a simultaneous shocked sucking in of breath and then a minor barrage of gasps, groans, and low-keyed shrieks, and terse exclamations that were a mixture of the religious and the obscene.

For Sam Colville, who would not have been able to sustain even his staggering gait had not Gomez been gripping him tightly around the upper arm, looked to be no more than a pathetic effigy of a man. Close to six feet tall, he could have weighed no more than ninety pounds, and those portions of his body and limbs that showed outside his slack-fitting underwear were little more than loose-hanging skin strung from the frame-work of bones. Much of the flesh that was on view was either scarred or festering and the stains on his pitifully inadequate clothing were a gory mixture of faded red blood and drab yellow pus. The thumbs of both his hands had been severed long enough ago for the stumps to have healed over. His left ear was missing too as was seen when his long hair—which would be silvery white when clean—swung to and fro with the lolling of his head as he was steered across the plaza by Gomez. His bare feet were as wasted as the rest of his physique, but showed no signs of torture below the ankles, which were marked with scars and recent wounds from iron shackles.

He made soft sounds that seemed at first to be gibberish. But when he was guided to within a few yards of the cantina doorway, Edge recognized a degree of form in the apparently meaningless babble. In the tension-filled silence of the night, before a horrified audience of which he seemed totally unaware, Sam Colville was using guttural, inarticulate sounds to ex-press the melody of "Marching Through Georgia."

"Does he not sing well in such unfortunate circum-stances?" Gomez asked rhetorically of the half-breed. And Colville's voice acted to trigger rasping sounds from the watchers, who vocalized the shock and revul-sion that showed on their faces. But this was abruptly silenced when the Federale officer glowered and roared harshly, "I have my position to maintain! If the Ameri-can had sung to the tune I wished to hear, his circum-stances would have been far more comfortable!"

"I was with Sherman on that march, feller," Edge said evenly, not needing to raise his voice since he was competing only with the inarticulate sounds made by the man whose attention he sought to draw.

Gomez and his prisoner were just a few feet from the threshold of the cantina now, and Colville heard the comment, staggered to a halt, and interrupted the melody as he brought his chin up off his chest. He held his head still for long seconds after Harriet Newton used a phrase Dinah McCall had so often spoken.

"Oh, my good Lord."

The man's face was almost fleshless, his skin draped over a grotesquely prominent bone structure into which his dark eyes were deeply sunken and his mouth seemed like a careless rip. The features were filthy dirty and thickly bristled. There were no teeth in his hanging-open mouth, and even the whites of his eyes were discolored.

"He understands nothing, señor," the Federale officer explained with a note of sadness that expressed no sympathy for the man he now urged forward. "Because of his own stupid stubbornness, he is now quite insane."

Just for an instant before the prisoner's head dropped forward and he again took up the Civil War marching song, Sam Colville seemed to contradict what Gomez had said as a glint of light showed in the former prisoner's eyes. But what this was intended to signify beyond signaling that Sam Colville's mind was perhaps still capable of rational thought, Edge could not tell. Maybe he had merely seen a reflection of the kerosene lamps above the bar at the rear of the cantina in the dead eyes of the tortured man.

The half-breed once again stepped out of the doorway to allow Gomez access to the area where the woman continued to experience horror and Delmar Pyle seemed once more to be struggling against the threat of nausea. But the uniformed man paused again, and while he retained his tight grip on Colville's arm, he used his free hand to force up the American's head and turn it so that the punished face was displayed for the audience on the plaza. Then, in a brutal tone he ordered the citizens of San Sarita to disperse and go about their evening business, advising them to look upon the *gringo* as a fine example of what could happen to anyone who did not respect his authority in this town.

He did not wait to witness the reaction to his command, but after the door was closed at his back, he undoubtedly heard the murmuring of angry voices and the reluctant shuffling of feet on the plaza as the crowd began to comply with his edict.

"This is Señor Sam Colville," Gomez announced, most of the harshness gone from his voice as he spoke again in American. "And in the faint hope that you will make me rich, I give him to you completely free."

"That can't be him," Delmar Pyle managed to squeeze out of his constricted throat as he rose to his feet again, slowly this time, using the table for support, his hands splayed on its top, his tattered title to half a gold claim between them.

"If he could talk, señor, he would most certainly tell you I do not lie."

Gomez continued to support Colville with his right hand beneath the American's left armpit. The Federale leaned comfortably against the wall to one side of the doorway while Edge stood a little away from the wall on the other side. Colville rested his back on the door between. He continued to have trouble carrying the familiar melody for more than a few moments at a time without faltering.

"But I was told he was no more than my age," Pyle argued. The defeated look on his face betrayed his conviction that he was contesting a lost cause.

"That is correct, señor," Gomez allowed, his composure completely returned following the flare of anger at the watchers out of the plaza. "As would have been self-evident had he not been so stubborn and had I not proved to be a man of honor who does not lie and who keeps his word."

The redhead who sat just ten feet in front of Gomez and Colville demanded, "For Pete's sake, cut all the crap and talk about what's important!"

"As you wish, señorita," the Federale answered evenly with a slight shrug of his broad shoulders. There was an abrupt end to Sam Colville's pathetic attempt to make the melody recognizable, and he began to utter quiet gibberish as Gomez explained tersely, "There have been rumors of a rich seam of gold in this area for many years. This man and another staked a claim to a section of the mountains where they were certain this bonanza was to be found. Because of my position here, I should know everything that occurs within my jurisdiction. Of the two men who claim to know the position of the rich seam of gold, one escaped north of the border. The second has since refused with increasing obstinacy to tell me what I should know."

Gomez spoke in the indifferent manner of a man explaining how he had attempted to overcome a minor obstacle to an unimportant goal. His voice was an unwavering monotone, and the look and sound of the man acted to intensify the horror that the woman was experiencing and to tighten the grip of desperation that held Pyle. Both of them were seeing the Mexican only on the unclear periphery of their vision as they stared at the muttering wreckage of a former man whose filthy flesh and clothing gave off a sickening stink. Edge thought he was perhaps the only person in the cantina to smell Colville, and he waited to hear something that might make him rich. He waited with faint hope, then became entirely concerned with staying alive, after he heard the strangely muffled sound of a revolver being cocked.

"I told him I was a vindictive man. I warned him that if he did not tell me what I wished to know, then he would not benefit from his knowledge himself. Nor would anybody else. I told him I would make him wish he was dead. And that is what I have done." Gomez shrugged as he paused in his dull-toned account. Colville abandoned his mutterings. "Do they not say that all brave men are fools? He has been brave, I cannot deny it. But it has made him worse than a fool. He is now an idiot, a raving lunatic who can do nothing but attempt to sing a soldier's song from—"

"No!" Delmar Pyle snarled, fighting despair with rage. "He's gotta tell us where it is! If he can't talk, he can show us!"

With one of his hands he snatched up the title paper while with the other he hurled the table out of his path. Now he came striding across the cantina, waving the paper frenetically as his swinging legs knocked aside other tables and chairs.

"Stay back!" Gomez snarled, surprised to near panic by the man's sudden moves. He snatched his hand down from supporting Colville to delve for the revolver under the flap of his hip holster.

The wasted man looked for just a moment as if he

were about to collapse, but then he uttered a fast but recognizable series of melodic notes which enabled him to hold on to his sanity for a few vital seconds.

On the other side of the doorway, Edge drew the ancient handgun from his holster and thumbed back the hammer as he powered into a half turn and went into a crouch, tracked the muzzle to aim at the Widow Banales, who stood in the archway behind the bar counter and drew from out of the folds of her loose-fitting dress the revolver that she had cocked within the sound-muffling fabric. The instant he saw the Mexican woman, grim resolution displacing grief on her careworn face, he recalled that moment when he had sensed something amiss on the plaza. Now he knew he had failed to see this woman among the crowd. But why should he have attached any importance to her absence, even if it had registered? There was no time now to analyze past events or the fact that the familiar Army model Remington in the two-handed grip of the Mexican widow woman explained why there was no such revolver in Harriet Newton's holster.

The redhead pleaded, "You can't, Edge!"

The Federale shrieked, *"Qué demonios?"*

Delmar Pyle roared, "Atta boy, Sam!"

Edge held his fire as he drew a bead on the widow, who swayed from side to side so that her aim was never steady on the back of Pyle, who in turn came to a skidding halt. He was as unaware of being threatened from behind as he doubtless had been that Gomez had intended to draw his revolver against him. The surprise that had interrupted anger within the Federale became sudden fear when the tortured Sam Colville turned toward him and snatched at the Colt before Gomez had got it clear of the holster.

Just for that moment—as the Mexican was surprised by the way the American folded away from the doorway and remained on his feet—the tortured man looked ineffectual and weak, and his thumbless, reaching hands seemed to need just a mere flick of the wrist by Gomez to knock them aside with the ease it would take to swat a fly. But then Colville's skeletal left hand fisted around the right wrist of Gomez while the Federale continued to feel surprise. The grip was tightened with a tremendous force born out of the insanity of the American. But this seeming proof that a man who loses his reason is compensated with an increase of brute strength was immediately denied when Sam Colville sang the wordless song louder than ever as he strove to hold on to sanity with the same tenacity as he gripped the wrist of his torturer. Then, to the encouragement of Delmar Pyle which he probably did not hear, Colville brought his right hand forward and snatched the revolver from the grasp of the Federale. To achieve this, he needed to use just limited strength, for Antonio Gomez emotions were crossing the line between surprise and fear, and it was not until a part of a second later that his mind would communicate to his physical being the need to retaliate.

"Da-da, da-da, da-da-da-da-da-da . . ." Sam Colville bellowed, and staggered backward, going between the wall and the back of Edge as he used the wrist of his left hand to knock back the hammer of the Federale's Colt.

"Please, you must not—"

Colville's skin-and-bone forefinger squeezed the trigger and he shot Antonio Gomez in the lower belly over a range of no more than four feet. The bullet dove deep inside the Mexican. Seeing that he could destroy the monster who had tortured him, Sam Colville cocked the hammer again and his finger squeezed the trigger. The second bullet drilled into the region of the Mexican's diaphragm as Gomez started down onto his knees, both hands pressed to the first blood-gouting wound. He screamed now, and the man who was killing him stopped singing, vented a sound that could have been laughter, then got the hammer back once more and squeezed the trigger a final time, blasting the bullet from the muzzle at the moment the Federale's knees impacted with the floor. His head was in line with the Colt, and this caused the bullet to tear into his temple as he turned his head and reached out a blood-dripping hand toward the door. The shot killed him, and the force of it through his head sent him toppling over backward off his knees.

The stink of drifting gunsmoke masked the stench of unclean flesh.

"Let's go, Sam!" Delmar Pyle roared, and made to step forward, waving his claim title like a celebratory banner as his very white teeth and his blue-green eyes glinted in a grin of triumph.

"*Bastardo!*" the Mexican woman behind the bar snarled the instant she was free of the state of debilitating fascination that had held her in its grip while she was witnessing the killing of the Federale captain. "*Le toca a usted!*"

Edge had kept his gun aimed at the Widow Banales and seen her gun in the double-handed grip at arm's reach as it wavered in the general direction of Pyle while her wide eyes were transfixed on the slaughter in the doorway.

"Let her, Edge!" Harriet Newton commanded, loud but ice cold.

The redhead's revolver was fired by the Mexican

woman, and the recoil of the big Remington sent the bullet high and wide. The half-breed held his fire.

"Lady, we can be rich!" Pyle bellowed, appearing irritated rather than afraid as he flung the words over his shoulder at the woman who cocked her gun in the open this time. He then switched his gaze to the half-breed and yelled, "Hey, let's get the hell out of here. Take Colville and—"

The Remington exploded again, and the second bullet cracked close enough to Pyle's head to fill him with the fear of death. He plunged forward again, desperate to reach the door, and the hand that had previously brandished the claim title in triumph now became part of the flailing arm that sent the redheaded woman staggering backward as she made to block his path.

Now Edge whirled around, still in the gunfighter's crouch. He was responding to the touch of something against the small of his back. Intent upon meeting a new danger, he raked his revolver away from the woman who posed no threat to him.

It had been the empty hand of Sam Colville that touched him to capture his attention. Colville displayed to the half-breed an expression that was akin to a smile as he used the Colt of the dead Federale officer in the manner of an orchestra conductor wielding a baton and began to *da-da-da* the marching song yet again.

There was a glint in his dark eyes once more, and this time Edge was able to meet the man's gaze for a whole second, which was long enough for him to guess that Sam Colville was expressing gratitude.

"Pleased to have helped you out," the half-breed told the wasted, near mindless man. Then found his attention snatched away from the grotesquely grinning face by a flurry of movement and a shattering sound.

He was in time to catch a fleeting, blurred glimpse of Delmar Pyle as the man lunged from a run into a dive that crashed him through the smashed window on the far side of the doorway.

A third wide-of-the-target shot from the big Remington in the hands of the widow sounded almost like an anticlimax after the crack of the breaking glass and the shriek from Delmar Pyle that may have been of triumph or agony.

Harriet Newton came painfully up off the floor where Pyle had knocked her and rasped bitterly, ''It was me you were hired to help, mister!''

Edge nodded as he listened to a babble of shouts and a clatter of running feet on the streets and the central plaza of San Sarita. Then, as he stooped to drag away the corpse of the Federale officer that had blocked Pyle's escape by the door, he said, ''Seems like the only jobs I ever get are the dead-end kind.''

''Still making jokes, tough guy!'' the redhead snarled as he pushed his gun into the holster before he swung wide the door. ''And that little shit is off and running again!''

''Mistakes get made, lady.''

''I sure as hell made one when I hired you! You had hopes for that gold mine story—''

''You were mistaken about Pyle,'' Edge cut in on her as he stepped out through the doorway.

His appearance against the lamplit interior of El Estelar Cantina caused the volume of sound and the level of movement to subside, the advance of the civilians and Federales to slow. Then all activity ended and the babble of talk lowered still more, when the slender form of the redhead was seen to emerge over the threshold, where she paused for a moment and caught her breath when she saw that Edge had gone down onto his haunches beside the prone body of Delmar Pyle. It was sprawled on the plaza amid a scattering of glass shards that gleamed brightly in the moonlight.

"Wrong about him being off and running, lady," Edge expanded.

Voices were raised again, demanding an explanation of what had been heard and seen of events in the cantina. Harriet Newton stepped closer to the half-breed so that he could hear her ask,

"Is he dead?"

The citizens of the town and the men from the Federale post grew subdued again when two more forms showed in silhouette at the cantina doorway. The Widow Banales needed to struggle to keep the no-longer-singing Sam Colville on his feet as she thrust the Remington toward the redhead, butt forward, saying, "*Muchas gracias, señorita.*"

Then, in a louder voice that gained in strength by the moment, she began a concise account of what had happened. Harriet Newton pushed the revolver back into her holster and said softly to Edge against the torrent of Mexican, "She asked me to loan her the gun, mister. For just in case she got a chance to kill the creep for what he did to her husband." She shrugged and glanced at the Widow Banales. "I couldn't have shot at him the way she did. But I guess it doesn't make any difference since she missed him. You didn't even try to shoot him."

Edge looked briefly at her and felt a mild twinge of pain between his eyes. He saw that her lean face beneath the peak of the forage cap showed even less reproach than had sounded in her voice as she finished saying her piece. He told her, "It was the widow woman who was most likely to kill me in there, lady."

She shrugged again and nodded, and it was as if she and Edge and the dead man stretched out before them were in a world apart from that in which the even-toned Widow Banales and the brutally tortured Sam Colville continued to hold the undivided attention of everyone else on the plaza.

"It's real strange," the redhead said dully. "There were so many people who wanted to kill him, and he killed himself in the end."

"No, lady," Edge murmured, and he touched with the tip of a long forefinger the largish shard of glass in the shape of a triangle that jutted out of the side of the neck of the inert man. His entire facedown head was surrounded by a huge stain of blood that the arid ground had not allowed to form into a pool. "Figure with all this blood, it must have cut into his jugular."

"What do you mean, no?" she asked.

"He got it in the neck," the half-breed murmured, and tapped the most damaging fragment of window glass before he withdrew his finger and started to unfold to his full height. "Not in the end. Which is where he ought to have got it, I figure."

Harriet Newton came upright beside him and growled, "For Pete's sake, mister!"

The Widow Banales was finished with her explanation and her listeners were stirring into movement again when Edge said evenly to the redhead, "Just that with a name like Pyle, it sounds like he should have got the pane in the ass."

Watch for

SHADOWS OF THE GALLOWS

next in the EDGE series
from Pinnacle Books

coming in February!

EDGE

George G. Gilman

More bestselling western adventure
from Pinnacle, America's #1 series publisher.
Over 8 million copies of EDGE in print!